THE ETERNAL POLICEMAN

robert l. bryan

Published by robert l. bryan, 2023.

THE ETERNAL POLICEMAN

First edition. July 25, 2023.

Copyright © 2023 robert l. bryan.

ISBN: 979-8223069751

Written by robert l. bryan.

For Meghan

CHAPTER 1: THE HEX

November 19th: The Christmas season in New York City was amazing. Even before New Yorkers digested their Thanksgiving turkey the atmosphere became indescribable, especially for those visiting the city for the first time. Countless lights and decorations seemed to be everywhere. The huge Christmas tree would soon be lit at Rockefeller Center and the window displays of the shops were being beautifully decorated. If there was something that really set the Christmas mood, it was the beautifully decorated streets and shop windows. Big department stores dedicated the whole year to preparing their Christmas windows, with each telling its own story. It was popular for both locals and tourists to wander past the stores during this period, especially on Fifth Avenue. The Radio City Christmas Spectacular starring The Rockettes provided one of the most iconic Christmas shows in New York, with Santa, the Nutcracker, and of course the Nativity.

The holiday season was also the busiest time of year for psychiatric hospitals where the spirit of the season only served to increase the depression of many suffering New Yorkers. All the bright, cheery holiday decorations could not mask the pain inside the psychiatric emergency room at Manhattan's Beth Israel Hospital.

Kyra took a deep breath and absorbed the quiet. After the initial surge of depression brought on by the upcoming holiday season, it was a rare calm evening in the psychiatric emergency room, and she had learned to savor these infrequent moments. As a second-year psychiatry resident, she had spent the better part of the previous year in the ER, with the normal working environment being the polar opposite of calm.

The locked 12-bed space was below capacity, with just six people dozing or quietly sitting on their beds. Unlike the day before, security guards didn't have to calm several agitated patients.

Kyra enjoyed the uncommon serenity as she walked from bed to bed during the first hour of her shift. She moved among the beds and staff, one eye on the clipboard and the other on her path. Kyra wore green scrubs with her black hair tied low in a pony-tail. She was Indian looking with large brown eyes, neatly lined in black. Kyra possessed the lithe movement of an athlete and the easy smile of one visiting a dear friend. She struck up conversations with each patient, assessing their moods and reassuring them that she was working to help them. She radiated compassion and confidence, even when one patient stepped uncomfortably close to her, clenching his fists by his sides.

Kyra noticed the patient's presence, but maintained her composure. "Hello, George, I'm Doctor Thomas."

"I can't take it in here," the large man sobbed, as a security guard quietly moved closer. The man didn't remember repeatedly punching the wall and failed to understand why his mother called the police, making him one of two involuntary admissions in the unit.

"We're really worried about you," Kyra explained. "Your mom is also worried about you." She told him he needed inpatient treatment, but that no beds were available yet. "We'll keep you posted and try to get you out of here soon."

After Kyra walked away, the man waited a few minutes, then ambled a little too casually toward the bathroom before dashing toward the doors leading out of the unit. The doors were locked, though, giving the same security guard time to approach and gently pick him up, pressing the patient's arms into his sides to lift him and carry him back to his bed.

Kyra gave only a brief glance to the escape attempt before moving on to another patient. This sixty-year old woman relied on the psychiatric emergency department for her medication management. She had bipolar disorder and a history of violence, and she sought help regularly when she was in danger of harming others.

Once the doctor was at her bedside, the woman showed Kyra a photo of her smiling granddaughter. "She's getting so big," Kyra cooed, able to chart the girl's growth after more than a year of progressive photos. Kyra squeezed the woman's hand gently. "Happy Holidays, Frances."

"You too, Dr. Thomas," the woman sang.

Kyra moved to the next bed and scanned her clipboard, noting the basic pedigree information – male, white, 24-years-old. "Well, I'm glad to see you're awake," she smiled.

Chris Bennington blinked and squinted, his eyes slowly coming to focus on the naked bulb above. He was dimly aware of his body being rigid and straight - no movement possible. Pulling his head upward he could see thick straps over his arms and legs. Saliva pooled in the back of his throat when he swallowed. More saliva came and over and over he drank it down so as not to panic. He twisted his limbs, turning them, feeling the friction of the fabric against his skin.

Chris rotated his head slowly. The room was windowless and dimly lit. He focused on the door without handles. Where was he? Deciphering the images would take some time, but one thing he was sure of. This was no ordinary hospital room. He tried to assess his situation. His mental functioning wasn't impaired. It was all about that bomb of information that had exploded in his head. The information had settled now and the pain was gone, but the memories were still vivid and frightening.

Chris laid his head back down on the pillow and focused on the smiling face above him. "You're a psychiatrist, aren't you?"

"Yes, I am, I'm Dr. Thomas."

Chris closed his eyes. "I'm not crazy, you know."

"I know that, Chris," Doctor Thomas smiled. "We're just trying to figure out what happened today."

"How long have I been here?" Chris gasped.

"A little over eight hours. You've been sleeping for a long time."

"Are my parents here?" Chris asked.

"They went home," Kyra replied. "Your condition was stable so I told them to go home and get some rest."

"Why am I strapped to the bed?"

"Hospital policy," she answered. "No big deal."

"Yeah, no big deal," Chris scoffed. "No big deal if you're a nut job."

"I know you're not crazy," Kyra assured. "But all your tests came back negative, so what happened to you this morning does not appear to be anything physical." She placed her hand on top of Chris's hand. "Trust me, Chris. I'm only trying to help you. I just want to find out what happened to you."

Chris laughed. "I know exactly what happened, but if I tell you you'll never let me out of these straps."

Kyra slid a chair next to the bed. "Tell me, Chris. Make me understand."

Chris bit his lip as he chose his words. "Do you have some memories that are very strong – very vivid?"

"Of course – it's normal for some events in life to leave lasting memories."

"Well," Chris continued. "I remember like it was yesterday when I hit a home run to win the championship game in the 7th grade, and I remember the first time I kissed a girl other than my mother."

"That's perfectly normal," Kyra chuckled.

Chris shook his head. "But I have more memories – memories that didn't exist until this morning – memories that aren't mine but suddenly exploded into my brain and are now as much a part of my life as that 7th grade home run." Chris sighed deeply. "It's alright doctor – I can see it in your eyes that you think I'm crazy, and frankly, if I were in your position I would think I'm crazy too."

"Tell me about these new memories," Kyra remarked. "Are these new memories important to you?"

"Important?" Chris snickered. "These new memories explain completely what happened to me and what is going to happen to me."

Kyra adjusted her position in the chair. "Tell me the story of your memories, Chris. Make me understand, too." She waited for Chris's response like she had all the time in the world and nothing could interest her more than what he had to say.

Chris Bennington looked up at Kyra through moist eyes. "This morning I fulfilled a lifelong dream – a dream that quickly turned into a nightmare."

"Tell me about your dream and nightmare."

Chris took a deep breath. "Ever since I could walk, I can remember wanting to be only one thing – a cop!"

"That's great," Kyra chimed in. "Do you have family members who are police officers?"

"No."

"How did your attraction to police work develop?" Kyra probed.

"I don't know," Chris lamented. "I've always wanted to be a cop and I don't know why? Crazy, right?"

"Not at all, Chris," Kyra reassured. "Many people have trouble pinpointing the origin of a career desire." She squeezed his hand. "It's okay. Continue with your story."

"After six long months at the police academy the day finally arrived. I stood with 852 fellow graduates in my immaculately pressed blue uniform creating a virtual sea of blue on the floor of Madison Square Garden." Chris paused for an instant. "Madison Square Garden," he repeated. "I was on the floor where I watched the Rangers and Knicks play. It was surreal."

"That must have been exciting," Kyra commented.

"Oh, it was," Chris agreed. "Especially when the moment arrived." Chris chuckled slightly. "Of course, we first had to endure a ten-minute rambling speech from the Mayor."

"I'm sure that was nice," Kyra interjected. "What did the Mayor say?"

Chris shrugged. "Who knows? I didn't hear a thing until he uttered the magic words."

"Magic words?"

Chris took another deep breath. "Please stand ladies and gentlemen while I administer the oath of office. I do solemnly swear that I will support the constitution of the United States, and the constitution of the State of New York, and that I will faithfully discharge the duties of the office of New York City Police Officer according to the best of my ability. So help me God." Chris's eyes widened. "And then he said, 'Congratulations officers.' I was an officer – everything was perfect. I took an oath. It was an oath that bound me to the other members of the department for life. It wasn't the kind of oath you made in front of some stuffy judge, it was the kind you made with spit and blood. It was the kind that made friends into brothers, the kind that transcended the mess of everyday life to strike an unbreakable bond."

"Wow, it does sound perfect," Kyra agreed.

Chris shook his head and bit his lip. "I got to enjoy the moment for all of about five seconds before it happened."

"What happened?"

"A sudden pounding headache and the feeling that all the air was leaving my lungs. I was taking frantic breaths, trying to keep myself calm. The information was overwhelming, like a huge wave pounding into the beach. I had never experienced anything like this before – the pounding – throbbing, like a toothache in my brain as all these vivid memories forced their way into my mind." Chris fished through his head for better words to explain. "It was like being blinded by lightning – flashes of white being all I could see – forcing me to shut my eyes and keep my eyes pressed into them. It was hell!"

Kyra gently stroked Chris's forearm. "I'm sorry this happened to you, Chris."

"My head throbbed," he continued. "The pain felt like someone had taken a knife to my skull. I squeezed my eyes shut and tried to will the pain to go away. The rest of the world became detached, all I could concentrate on was the pain rooted deep in my head caused by the overload of foreign information pouring into my brain. I could barely hear my classmates chattering around me. They were all around me but then they seemed to be floating above me. They had not levitated, but I didn't even realize I was lying on the floor." Chris shrugged. "My position was incidental information. All I felt – all I knew was the pain of the moment." He glared up at the bulb on the ceiling. "And then I was here – with you and generations of new memories."

"Tell me about these memories, Chris."

Chris smiled. "I'll tell you everything, doctor, but you better get comfortable because I have to start in the 17th century – in 1692 to be specific."

The Memories of Chris Bennington

1692: It was not yet noon when the clouds gave of their rain to the grass and trees. For Baltis Van Steyer, there was no time to appreciate any beauty in nature. The dirt road had transformed into mud and he had to trudge a quarter mile ankle deep in the muck before reaching the shelter of the "Stadt Huys" or City Hall as it was then called. In the basement of the building were cells for prisoners, who were mainly unruly sailors from ships in the harbor.

Van Steyer's mood was as dark as the sky as he grabbed a large key from a peg on the wall and carefully strode down the winding stone steps. On this late morning the cell in the basement contained one occupant. Baltis Van Steyer stepped inside the dark, dirty cell and faced the seated prisoner.

"I take no joy in these proceedings, madam, but as high constable of New York I have been charged with a duty and I shall carry out that duty."

•••

In 1658, Peter Van Steyer was making his way in the New World. A carpenter by trade, Peter had made the voyage to New Amsterdam with his wife in 1653. He built a small cottage in the settlement and made his living not as a carpenter, but as a wheelwright. Then, as now, everyone needed wheels, whether for wagons, wheelbarrows, or dung carts, and these conveyances were in reliable need of repair on a regular basis. New Amsterdammers like Van Steyer worked hard at their chosen occupations, and cannily used their real estate to feather their nests. They were situated firmly in what might be called today the middle class of New Amsterdam. By 1658 Van Steyer had the financial means to buy land on Manhattan just south of the wall, the northern boundary of New Amsterdam.

The dreams of the New World were becoming a reality for the Van Steyer's. With a good trade and a well-built home, the only thing missing was an addition to the family. In 1660 Baltis Van Steyer completed the family unit.

Peter Stuyvesant could make life miserable for those he didn't like, but as Peter Van Steyer learned, misery could also come from the governor's affection. Unhappy with the workmanship on a bedroom in his mansion, Stuyvesant tasked an aid to find a highly skilled carpenter to complete the work in his home. The aid stopped to admire the exquisite workmanship on a cottage just south of the wall and two days later Peter Van Steyer labored in the governor's mansion.

In a rare display of affection, Peter Stuyvesant was immediately fond of the affable Van Steyer. This relationship with the governor did Peter no good, however, for with the time he spent toiling for the governor he earned less than with his wheelwright trade. Over the next several months Peter worked various odd jobs and projects for the governor and expected no reward. In fact, Peter simply wanted to be free to resume his wheelwright trade without interruption. So, it was with a substantial lack of enthusiasm that Peter Van Steyer reacted to the governor's latest edict.

9

Because of the high regard in which he was held. Peter Van Steyer was appointed captain of the Rattle Watch. Such an appointment was the last thing Peter desired, but he knew that a smart man never said no to Governor Peter Stuyvesant. In essence, Peter Van Steyer had become New York City's first chief of police.

Then in 1664, England claimed all of New Netherlands, including New Amsterdam, and four warships with nearly 500 soldiers bore down on New Amsterdam. Peter Stuyvesant had hoped to resist the English, but being an unpopular ruler, his Dutch subjects refused to rally around him. Following its capture, New Amsterdam's name was changed to New York, in honor of the Duke of York, who organized the mission. When the City passed to English control, the English and Dutch settlers lived together peacefully. Under British rule constables were charged with keeping the peace, focusing on such offenses as excessive drinking, gambling, prostitution, and church service disturbances. In 1664 Peter Van Steyer's title was changed to High Constable of New York.

Nepotism was common in English culture at the time, so it was no surprise that in 1692, thirty-two year old Baltis Van Steyer was the High Constable of New York.

Despite being under English rule, New York maintained much of its Dutch identity. Before ceding power, Peter Stuyvesant managed to get in writing the Articles of Capitulation, which gave the Dutch population civil rights and freedom of religion, rather than being forced like all other British colonies to convert to the Anglican church.

The Dutch founded villages on Long Island: Bushwick, Brooklyn, Flatbush, and Flatlands. When the British captured the Dutch territory in 1674, they gathered the villages into Kings County, part of the crown colony of New York. In 1692 Katherine Harris was a widowed landowner with three children living on her farm in Kings County.

Harris was a local healer, known for her abilities for curing diseases. Fueled by a dispute over money, many of her neighbors began to suspect that she was using her magic to cause physical harm and even death.

English witchcraft traditions held that with the devil's help, witches could change their appearance, or appear to be in two places at once. The apparition was often thought to be the devil himself, assuming the shape of his partner witch. At least three people swore they had seen the specter of Katherine Harris.

Armed with a warrant signed by the Chief magistrate of New York, High Constable Baltis Van Steyer ferried to Kings County and took custody of Katherine Harris. Harris was found guilty of witchcraft and sentenced to death by hanging at the gallows erected near the cage and stocks on Dock Street.

...

Thunder rolled across the dark skies as Baltis Van Steyer bent over to grab the arm of the seated prisoner. He had not taken much notice of the condemned during the journey from Long Island, but now, minutes before her demise, Baltis felt compelled to study the unfortunate woman.

The accused witch scowled into the gloom and ran her boney hand through the thatch of greying black hair on her head. The effect was to make her look more deranged. The hair had been hacked in random stabbing motions, presumably by the neighbors whose accusations had brought her to this end. Beneath the crude mop was a face less appealing. Over the past half century her skin had become crusty, falling off in flakes the size of almond slices. Her mouth had puckered from lack of smiling. She was, however, incredibly quiet. Baltis was wary of her silence, sensing it was something she used to her advantage when seeking subjects for her sorcery – catching her victims unaware whilst they struggled to breathe in her stench.

"It's time ma'am," he whispered. "And may God have mercy on your wretched soul."

With the aid of the constable's arm Katherine Harris pulled herself upright. She kept a firm grip on Van Steyer's hand and glared into his eyes. The icy stare unsettled Baltis and he once again felt the need to qualify his actions. "There is no joy for me in this day, but I am the King's servant with a duty to uphold, and on this day I fulfill my duty with regrets."

Baltis attempted to release his grip but Katherine's hand remained tightly clasped around his. Her icy stare matched the tenor of her words. "Hear me ye servant of the king performing ye dark duty. From this day forward ye will be cursed by ye duty and oath. Ye duty shall be thy demise in this existence and existence for all time. Ye rotten soul will drift from duty to duty, from oath to oath – all with the same end – death."

...

1701: Thomas Anderson had work to do. There was always work to be done on his Kings County farm, but on this late morning he had returned to his modest cottage without completing his labor in the fields. His entry into the one-room dwelling found his wife Martha sweeping the wooden plank floor. Before she could express any surprise by his presence, Thomas grabbed her by the waist, pulling her up close against his chest. His hand gently glided through her hair, as he peered into her eyes in a way he seldom looked at her. Her eyes were candles in the dim light of the room, their light a spark of passion... desire. As a small but teasing smile crept upon her face, goosebumps lined her skin, not the kind that one gets in the cold, but the kind one gets when nothing else matters except right here, right now. The farm, his unfinished work and the rest of his world for that matter became an unimportant blur that was banished into the far recesses of his mind. The only thing that mattered was touching her more, kissing her mouth, her stomach, her breasts. He tried to be gentle with her clothing, not to rip the lace, but it was hard. His hands were made for chopping wood and sowing the land rather than intimate passion.

There was an exhilaration Baltis Van Steyer had not experienced in many months. He had no explanation for it, but as he ambled along Maiden Lane with the sun light painting his skin so warmly, the trees seemed to take the form of dancing ladies, each in dresses more fabulous than he had ever seen. They moved, choreographed by the wind, in perfect time with one another. They were the life and soul of this early summer morning, and the fuel for his bliss. As the trees stretched their limbs upwards and outwards toward the light, drinking in rays as pure as the rain, Baltis stretched his arms too, fingers spread toward the sun. His high spirit could not be dashed, not even by Jonas Wolff.

At one time, Jonas Wolff had been a sailor with the Dutch East India Company. A freak accident with a bow line had severed his right leg below the knee leaving him with a wood peg to replace the limb. In the two

13

years since the accident Jonas split his time between begging on the street, drunkenness, and residing in the basement jail cell of the Stadt Huys. The High Constable had arrested Jonas Wolff at least a dozen times so the action on this morning was nothing more than routine.

Mary Bogaert was pacing outside her cottage north of the wall. When she spied the High Constable coming down the lane she advanced to meet him. "He has been there all night," she lamented.

Baltis nodded. "I know. John Langdon sought me out and made the complaint an hour ago."

Mary pointed to her garden and the rows of meticulously maintained tulip bulbs. "He's ruining my flowers."

Baltis smiled at the irate woman. "Stay calm madam. I will be on my way with him in tow momentarily."

Baltis strode carefully into the garden, careful not to upset any flowers. Jonas Wolff lay face down among the tulips, slaying at least eight bulbs. Baltis kicked the bottom of Wolff's boot. "Come lad. You've caused this good woman enough concern. Let's be moving and you can find your rest in your usual spot."

The moaning and slow stirring was normal as was the slow rise to an upright position. What wasn't normal was the sword clasped in the right hand of Jonas Wolff. Without word or warning the sabre crashed down on the neck of High Constable Baltis Van Steyer, almost severing his head.

Martha Anderson looked forward to her monthly trek to Manhattan. She enjoyed everything about the journey – the ferry, the market, socializing with ladies of her acquaintance, and especially the broadside. Martha scanned the broadside and found her attention drawn to the paper on the center of the board. It was a proclamation from the governor.

Let it be known by all that with heavy heart I announce the death of Baltis Van Steyer, High Constable of New York and loyal servant of the King. The High Constable, falling victim to murder while maintaining his royal oath in performance of his duties.

Although Martha did not know Baltis Van Steyer, as she read the proclamation she experienced a strange sensation in her stomach. This was not a reaction to the news on the proclamation. Although she had never experienced this feeling before, she needed no doctor's explanation. Every woman instinctively recognized the tingling of life.

•••

By 1728 the Dutch Stadt Huys had been replaced by a new City Hall on Wall and Nassau Streets. There was a general disinterest to the proceedings taking place on the steps of the new government building. Men and women scurried about absorbed in their business of the day. Only Thomas and Martha Anderson stood proudly at the bottom of the stairs looking up to Mayor Robert Lurting, captivated by the ceremony.

Mayor Lurting handed a scroll to the man standing to his right. "Read the oath," he directed.

John Anderson unrolled the parchment and cleared his throat. "I do solemnly and sincerely declare and affirm that I will well and truly serve the King in the office of constable, cause the peace to be kept and preserved and prevent all offences against people and property; and that while I continue to hold the said office I will to the best of my skill and knowledge discharge all the duties thereof faithfully according to the law of the Crown."

The mayor took the scroll in his left hand and placed his right hand on John's left shoulder. "Go forth and serve thy King and people well, Constable John Anderson."

John nodded and smiled at the Mayor and then to his parents. The grin suddenly transitioned to a look of concern and confusion. John blinked and jerked his head backwards with each flash. It was like quick jolts of lightning in his brain, and then it was gone. The smile returned as John descended the steps of City Hall and embraced his parents.

On the ferry returning to Kings County, Thomas Anderson draped his arm around his son's shoulder as they stared out to the calm river waters. "Your mother and I are very proud of you today, constable."

John nodded and continued to stare at the calm waters. The concerned look had returned to his face as he turned to address his father. "I need to tell you something," John began. "Something happened during the ceremony that I do not understand."

"What happened, son?"

"When I completed my oath, it was as if bolts of lightning struck my head."

Thomas Anderson chuckled. *"That was just the excitement of being appointed a constable of the King."*

John shook his head. *"No, father, there is more. After I felt the jolts, something very strange happened."*

"What happened."

"My brain was filled with memories that were not my own."

"I don't understand, son."

"Nor do I, father, but do you have knowledge of a citizen named Baltis Van Steyer?"

Thomas Anderson stroked his chin. *"Baltis Van Steyer...the name is familiar. Yes, yes this man was High Constable of New York some twenty or thirty years past."*

"Do you know what became of him?" John asked.

"Yes," Thomas nodded. *"He met a tragic end – murdered by a hooligan while performing his duty."*

John stared deeply into his father's eyes. *"High Constable Baltis Van Steyer was murdered on July 15th, 1701 by Jonas Wolff. Van Steyer had arrested Wolf many times earlier for drunkenness and was attempting to do the same when he was felled by a blow from Wolff's sword."*

"How do you know this?" Thomas gasped.

"This is not all I know," John continued. *"Baltis Van Steyer was cursed by a witch for carrying out his duty, with the curse said to carry on through all time to others who take an oath to fulfill their solemn duty."*

Thomas Anderson grabbed his son's forearm tightly. *"Speak no more like this. You have heard the tale of the unfortunate High Constable throughout the years in our own home. It was your mother who brought the story to us when she read the governor's proclamation."* Thomas gritted his teeth and his voice became no more than a whisper. *"Now say no more on this lest people believe you are bewitched."*

Thomas Anderson released his grip on his son and they resumed their silent study of the still waters.

•••

One of the more productive farms in the City was owned by George McFarland. McFarland, a widower, worked his farm on Bowry Road alone. George McFarland was a serious man consumed with his work, and little more. On this day, however, agriculture was not on his mind. Eighteen-year old Clara McFarland was to be wed to Peter Forsythe, a British merchant seaman who had fallen in love with Clara and was giving up life at sea to work the farm with George McFarland.

An Anglican Minister made the two-mile journey from Lower Manhattan to the McFarland farm to perform the ceremony, a ceremony that included reading the Book of Common Prayer with its familiar words that begin *dearly beloved, we are gathered together here in the sight of God, and in the face of this congregation, to join together this man and this woman in holy matrimony.* Along with these familiar words came familiar acts as well. George McFarland gave his daughter away, the couple exchanged vows, and the groom gave the bride a ring. The bride, however, did not present a ring to the groom.

Just as it does today, a party began after the ceremony. This celebration also took place at the McFarland home. A table was decorated with white paper chains and laid out with white foods for collation. The food included two white cakes. The guests consumed the groom's cake, and left the bride's cake untouched for the couple to save in a tin of alcohol to eat on each wedding anniversary.

There was much food, drink, and toasting along with games and plenty of dancing. Eventually, the bride and groom retired to the privacy of a specially prepared bedroom to share intimacy for the first time.

While Peter and Clara were enjoying the flames of their new marital relationship, flames of a literal type were turning the night to day at Fort George on the southern tip of the City. Crimson anger arose from the burning house of Governor George Clark. The fury of the flames burst out *as it devoured the wood hungrily expressing all its rage and wrath. Smoke released out of the flames and boyishly danced around the building.*

The Governor and an entourage of onlookers watched from a distance as the great mansion went up in flames. Soon the church connected to the house was ablaze too. People tried to save it but the fire soon grew beyond control. The flames leaped and danced as they consumed, radiantly beautiful in their destruction. Fresh embers jumped and spread ever higher until both structures were completely engulfed in a blazing inferno.

It was unclear where the information originated, but suddenly the onlooking crowd was frantic with word of a child being trapped inside the burning church. Constable John Anderson left Governor Clarke's side to rush into the flames. There was no child inside the church and John Anderson never came out.

···

Chris paused and smiled. "I could go on in minute detail for several more hours, but I think you get the picture. The names, dates, and titles have changed but the story is always the same. In 1776 it was Constable James Forsythe, and 1825 George Muldoon. In 1881 Police Officer Seamus O'Toole met his fate followed by Henry Swanson in 1930."

Doctor Thomas fidgeted in her chair. "Forgive me Chris – I'm trying to understand this. Are you theorizing that all these officers were the victim of some type of curse that originated in 17th century New Amsterdam?"

Chris stared at the light bulb in the ceiling. "At the risk of getting more restraints placed on me I'm just saying what I know."

"And how exactly did you arrive at this theory?"

Dr. Thomas recoiled at Chris's volume. "It's not theory," he bellowed. "It's fact! And it's fact because I remember every detail."

"And you remember every detail from people who lived in the 17th century?"

Chris shook his head and laughed. "This is ridiculous. I should have just kept my mouth shut and answered more of those questions like who is the President of the United States. Now, you're never gonna let me out of here, are you?"

Kyra placed her hand back on Chris's. "Please, Chris. I'm not the enemy. Finish you story."

Chris took a deep breath. "After Harry Swanson there was Joe Martino in 1972 and then Charles Johnson in 1996."

"And all of these people were policemen in New York City who were killed in the line of duty?"

"That's right," Chris nodded, "and now it's me."

Dr. Thomas smiled. "But you're alive."

Chris closed his eyes. "You just don't get it. When Baltis Van Steyer was cursed in 1692 he was destined to die in the line of duty. When Jonas Wolff brought his sword down on Van Steyer's neck, across the river in Kings County Martha and Thomas Anderson were conceiving John Anderson. When Van Steyer died the curse jumped to a newly conceived life. From that instant John Anderson was destined to be a policeman and he was condemned to die in the line of duty."

"Did he die in the line of duty?" Doctor Thomas asked.

"In 1742 – in a fire in the Governor's mansion, at the same moment James Forsythe was conceived."

"James Forsythe was one of the names you mentioned," Dr. Thomas remarked.

"That's right," Chris continued. "Forsythe, Muldoon, O'Toole, Swanson, Martino, Johnson, and now me."

Dr. Thomas shrugged. "But if they all knew they were going to die on the job why did they become policemen?"

"Because the memories are not acquired until the oath of office is taken. The moment I put my right hand down my brain exploded with all these memories of these men. Memories that are now part of me."

Dr. Thomas stroked her chin. "So, all these men knew they were destined to die in the line of duty after they took the oath. Why didn't they try to do something about it?"

"The officers in the 17th and 18th centuries were afraid of being caught in the net of witchcraft themselves. The other ones just ignored it – all except Johnson."

"What happened with Johnson?" the doctor asked.

"Charles Johnson was born on October 10, 1972. Police Officer Joe Martino was killed in a gun battle in Brooklyn on February 3, 1972."

"So how did this curse transfer?" Dr. Thomas cut in. "the dates are different."

"Johnson was born on October 10th, but he was conceived on February 3rd, the same day Martino was killed in the line of duty."

Dr. Thomas squinted and tilted her head slightly. "So, in 1996, Johnson was still very young when he was killed. He couldn't have been a police officer very long."

"You're right," Chris agreed. "Johnson was the one officer in the line who tried to do something about it."

"What did he do?"

"Johnson graduated from the academy on July 7, 1996. When he took the oath of office all the memories I received poured into his brain. He realized right at the graduation ceremony that he was a condemned man, so he thought that if he quit the job immediately he could somehow break the curse."

"So, he quit right there?" Dr. Thomas asked.

"He tried to quit right there at Madison Square Garden, but the lieutenant from academy recruit operations thought he was crazy and dismissed him by saying that if he really wanted to quit he should go to the Personnel Bureau at One Police Plaza and resign."

"What did he do?"

"He took the lieutenant's advice. "He jumped on a subway train to go to police headquarters, but he never made it."

"What happened?"

When he stepped into the A train at 34th Street, he stepped right into the middle of an armed robbery taking place. Shots were exchanged and when it was over the perpetrator was wounded, but Charles Johnson had been killed in the line of duty." Chris nodded. "That was July 7th, 1996. I was born on April 4th, 1997, but I was conceived on July 7th, 1996."

Dr. Thomas squeezed Chris's hand. "Don't worry, Chris. I'm not going to let anything happen to you."

"Have you not heard a word I said?" Chris exclaimed. "My fate is sealed. Unless there is some way to remove this curse, I will die in the line of duty whether it is tomorrow or thirty years from now."

"What if you never get to work as a police officer?" the doctor asked.

"Then you'll be signing my death warrant," Chris responded.

"What do you mean?"

"If you find me psychologically unfit to be a police officer and I get fired or put out on a medical disability, before I'm separated from the department something will happen. Maybe I'll push a child out of the way of a speeding car and get killed, or maybe I'll drown trying to save a swimmer who fell into the river. I don't know," he shrugged, "but I do know that before my separation papers get signed, I will be killed under circumstances that will be considered a line of duty death."

"This is a lot to digest, Chris." Dr. Thomas rubbed the back of his hand. "I'm going to let you rest for a while. I'm sure your parents will be in to see you shortly and I'll be back tomorrow to check in on you."

"Thank you for listening doctor," Chris squeezed her hand. "And please don't let them terminate me off the job until I can try to figure this out. Remember, the moment I'm off the job I'll be dead."

Dr. Thomas pulled her hand away while trying to appear unconcerned. "I'll see you tomorrow, Chris."

CHAPTER 2: COULD IT BE TRUE?

Professor Linda Warren had lost interest in the current speech. She was the next scheduled speaker, but all she could think about was water. She desperately waved to get a waiter's attention until she finally caught the eye of a fast-moving young server, and a minute later she was clearing her throat with a much-needed cold drink. Although interested in the topic for many years, the conference on modern witchcraft was the first time Professor Warren had been a public speaker on the subject, and she found herself unexpectedly nervous while waiting to speak.

The two hundred guests mostly represented academia from the northeast United States and Canada. As Linda drained her water glass and scanned the ball room, she noted the elegant décor. The grand ballroom in Manhattan's luxurious Four Seasons Hotel was truly awe inspiring, with finely adorned tables, 35-foot ceilings, turn-of-the-century teardrop chandeliers, blonde hardwood floors, a horseshoe-shaped balcony, and a built-in stage. Linda allowed herself a moment of fantasy to visualize her own wedding in these exquisite surroundings. Her own laughter brought her back to reality. There was no way she and Kyra could afford anything close to this room.

The polite applause signaled that the speaker from New York University was done with his remarks. Linda fidgeted in her chair as the master of ceremonies read a very complementary introduction. As the applause resonated, Professor Warren collected her notes and moved behind the ornate wooden podium. Despite drinking so much water, she still had to clear her throat several times before commencing her speech.

"Forty years ago, a group of protesters calling themselves witches staged a Halloween 'hex' on Wall Street. Dressed in all black, with long peaked hats, the women sneaked through the narrow streets of downtown Manhattan late into the night, making their way to the entrance to the New York Stock Exchange, where they oozed glue into the latches of its doors. The next morning, the male bankers couldn't get in — and the Dow reportedly fell 13 points. This hex that effected the stock market was about as real as it gets. In other words – it's nonsense. The market fell that day because of the inability of the personnel to access the building, not because of a magic spell." Linda paused for a moment to allow the sporadic laughter to cease. "Today, there might be no need to sneak around. Real witches are roaming among us, and they're seemingly everywhere. Haven't you noticed? Witches are your millennial co-workers doing tarot card readings on their lunch breaks, and professional colleagues encouraging you to join them for a New Moon ceremony aimed at career success. Witches are influencers who use hashtags to share horoscopes, spells and witchy memes, and they are panelists and podcasters." Linda paused for a sip of water. "Yes, it seems the time has come for witches to come out of the so-called broom closet. Witchcraft is all about empowering women. We're in a period of great transition, and we're all very aware of it. There's an increase of globalization, an enormous amount of polarization, and for many people, spirituality is speaking to them -it's giving them autonomy. And, of course, witches have long been linked to women's issues, which are front and center in the present political moment. I often say, show me your witches and I'll show you your feelings about women. Witches reflect our fears and our fantasies about women with power." Linda took a deep breath as she scanned her audience. "Witchcraft can be a powerful positive force, especially for women, and while I remain open to the existence of real magic," She shook her head. "But spells and hexes – I think not."

Kyra's routine after an evening in the ER was to stagger into her apartment and head directly to the bedroom and some much-needed sleep. On this night, however, she broke from the norm. Instead of jumping under the blankets she stretched her legs out on the living room sofa and enjoyed a glass of wine and the view of the Manhattan skyline afforded from her 14th floor Long Island City building. It wasn't the less hectic pace of the shift that supplied Kyra with this burst of energy, it was Chris Bennington. She sipped her wine and shook her head. This was absurd and she knew it. She was a medical professional – a psychiatrist. She heard all types of delusional tales from patients during her residency, so what was different about this one. It certainly wasn't his description of witchcraft and curses. Kyra had no time for people who believed in such nonsense. Yet, there was something different about Chris. There was no physical or psychological ailment found to explain his new memories, and they were so vivid – filled with such detail. Regardless of how absurd it was, she could not get Chris Bennington's story out of her mind. She couldn't wait to brief Linda. Who better to provide insight into this incredible tale than a professor of early American History at Columbia University. A professor who was also extensively well read and written on the topics of witchcraft and the occult.

Kyra turned toward the apartment door at the sound of the key turning. "Hey babe," she grinned, her legs curled underneath her on the sofa. "I have to tell you about one of my patients today."

Professor Linda Warren was having none of it. Without uttering a word, the tall, slim, blonde, 35-year old placed her bag on the countertop and smiled as she approached Kyra. Linda gently touched her forehead to Kyra's. Kyra could feel Linda's breath fanning her face, and she began to quiver when Linda slowly began to run her nose up and down and along the side of Kyra's nose. Suddenly, Kyra's agenda didn't seem so important. Her hand slipped around the back of Linda's neck and very gently she pulled her in closer until their mouths met. Simultaneously, both mouths opened, their tongues playfully testing each other. Linda's tongue was everywhere, probing every inch of Kyra's mouth. Her hand found its way to Kyra's shoulder, her thumb sweeping over the side of her throat. Kyra maintained the lip lock as she grabbed Linda's hand from her neck and rose from the sofa. She squeezed Linda's hand gently as she led her lover across the living room and through the bedroom door. Chris Bennington's curse had been around since 1692, another hour wasn't going to matter.

Linda lay on her back in the king size bed., feet twitching to music only she could hear, her face as passive as it would be in slumber. Kyra moved closer, lying on her side gently twirling Linda's long blonde hair in her fingers. Though she was already awake, Linda opened her eyes as if from a deep sleep and smiled. "You have completely worn me out, girlfriend."

"I'm that good?" Kyra laughed.

"Your beautiful body all over me was enough," Linda explained. "But this story about your cursed patient was just too much to absorb."

Kyra plopped down on her back. "You don't believe me."

Linda rose up on her right elbow. "Oh, I believe you, babe – but the story – come on." She gently stroked Kyra's left cheek. "My God, you're a psychiatrist. I thought you learned all about delusional people."

Kyra stared at the bedroom ceiling. "You're probably right." She shook her head. "But there was just something different about the way he told the story – something very genuine."

Linda shrugged. "Some of the most disturbed people are also the most manipulative – you told me that."

Kyra turned her head on the pillow to face Linda. "And witchcraft is not necessarily all fairytales – you told me that."

Kyra closed her eyes and placed her head on Linda's shoulder, breathing deeply and enjoying the serenity.

Suddenly, Linda sat up in bed. "Would I be able to interview your patient?"

"Now, you're interested," Kyra chuckled.

"I've been on the tenure track for two years," Linda replied. "Dr. Westbrook told me just last week that I better think about getting published."

"That shouldn't be a problem for you," Kyra said. "You like all this research stuff."

"That true," Linda sighed. "I just need the topic and the time. In addition to my coursework, I have to advise freshman, supervise independent studies and senior theses."

"I thought you liked your advisory role."

"I do," Linda confirmed. "It's among the most satisfying parts of the job, but it's also very time consuming. And now," she continued, "with higher education getting increasingly competitive, there are very few colleges and universities that are not keenly interested in their relative status and prestige. And Dr. Westbrook is convinced that the key to increasing an institution's visibility and ability to attract good students is the reputation of its faculty as reflected by publications."

Linda turned on her side and planted a quick kiss on Kyra's lips. "And here comes my special girl to save the day."

"I wouldn't say I saved the day," Kyra scoffed. "I just know you are into this kind of stuff."

Linda pecked Kyra's lips again and shook her head. "No, babe, you are a lifesaver. I have been racking my brain for a topic I can get published, and you come home and drop it in my lap."

"What topic?"

"The effect of witchcraft in Colonial New York City. There's been oodles of research on witchcraft in New England and the Salem Witch Trials, but I can't recall any scholarly works regarding New York City during the same period."

"Do you think you're going to get a complete publication from a meeting with my patient?"

"Of course not," Linda laughed. "But meeting Mr. Chris Bennington might be a very good starting point for my project, and more importantly, it will give me the motivation to actually get started."

"I'll have no trouble arranging your meeting," Kyra said. "I just have to get his permission, but I'm sure he'll agree to it."

"Great," Linda responded.

"But you better come tomorrow," Kyra warned.

"Why?"

"Aside from this event that occurred to him with all these new memories he claims to have, there's nothing wrong with Chris, and he's definitely not a danger to himself or others."

"And your point?" Linda probed.

"My point is that Chris will be with us for only two more days at the most, and there is a chance he could be discharged tomorrow."

"I'll be there tomorrow afternoon," Linda smiled as her lips moved towards Kyra's mouth.

•••

November 20th: "Hey," Kyra nodded as she came out to the ER waiting room. "Sorry about the wait, but I had to finish with a patient."

"No problem," Linda replied. "Where is my interviewee."

"Chris is in another building," Kyra stated. "He's going to be discharged tomorrow so they moved him into the Jonas Pavilion until then. It's a low security ward."

Linda stopped as they turned up the walkway to the building. "Oh my God!" she gasped.

"What?"

Linda pointed to a slab of concrete next to the entrance door. "Look at that."

"What about it?" Kyra responded.

"It says Jonas Asylum."

"I know," Kyra shrugged. "That's what the name used to be."

Linda shook her head. "That term 'asylum' – isn't it a bit jarring."

"What do you mean?"

"Think about it," Linda began. "Places like this are not consistent with the meaning of the word. Is this really a place to seek asylum? It should be a place of refuge from the storms that hurt the mind, a place of love and sanctuary, a place to be welcomed into arms that will hold you until the entire self is soothed, content simply to dwell in those moments with you, being your anchor, the pillar in your hurricane."

Kyra took a deep breath. "I really can do without the dramatics right now."

Kyra led Linda to a table in a large day room. "Chris will be out here in a couple of minutes."

Linda took in the entire room and shook her head. "These bare walls and bare floors are reflections of what this place really is, as if the building itself was trying to tell the staff what they had built and

31

perpetuated. And the lack of windows and real light, it is the world's most obvious constructed metaphor for emotional indifference."

"Please stop," Kyra whispered. "Here he comes."

Linda and Kyra stood as Chris approached. Linda was surprised to see him wearing a sweatshirt and jeans in lieu of a hospital gown.

"Hi Chris," Kyra greeted.

Chris smiled. "Hi Dr. Thomas."

Kyra extended her arm toward Linda. "This is Linda Warren, the person I said wanted to talk to you."

Chris extended his arm for a handshake. "Hi, Professor Warren. Dr. Thomas has told me a lot about you."

"All good, I hope," Linda chuckled. "And please, none of that professor nonsense. My name is Linda."

"I guess you'll be happy to get out of here," Kyra said. "Is it tomorrow?"

"Not soon enough," Chris commented. "But I still have that whole other issue to deal with," he sighed.

Kyra placed her hand on Chris's left shoulder. "Well, that's what professor....I mean Linda wants to talk to you about." Kyra guided Chris down in the chair. "I have to get back to the ER so I'll leave you two to talk."

Chris turned to watch Kyra leave through the door. "Dr. Thomas is great," Chris commented. "She's the only good thing that has happened to me here." He turned in his chair to face Linda. "Are you and Dr. Thomas good friends?"

Linda smiled. "I guess you could say that."

Chris slapped his hands down on the table. "So, what can I tell you, Linda?"

"I don't know how much Dr. Thomas told you, so let me start by giving you a little about my background. I am a professor of Early American History at Columbia University, and I have also done a lot of study on the subject of witchcraft in Colonial America."

Chris nodded. "that's what Dr. Thomas told me."

"I want to be up front with you, Chris," Linda continued. "I hope I'm able to help you, but this interview will benefit me."

"How?" Chris asked.

"I need to get published as part of my tenure requirements, and I am trying to author a scholarly paper on witchcraft in colonial New York."

Chris shrugged. "I will do whatever I can to help you."

"Thanks," Linda nodded. "Dr. Thomas told me your basic story about your memories that date back to the 17th century. I want to start by trying to fill in some gaps."

"Go ahead."

"From what I understand, your first memories are of a Van Steyer family, is that correct?"

"Correct."

"Do you know how the Dutch came to New York, or New Amsterdam at the time?"

Chris shook his head. "I haven't got a clue."

"On September 2, 1609, Englishman Henry Hudson, in the employ of the Dutch East India Company, sailed the Half Moon through the Narrows into Upper New York Bay. Like Christopher Columbus, Hudson was looking for a westerly passage to Asia. He never found one, but he did take note of the abundant beaver population. Beaver pelts were in fashion in Europe, fueling a lucrative business. Hudson's report on the regional beaver population served as the impetus for the founding of Dutch trading colonies in the New World, and in particular, the Dutch settlement of New Amsterdam. New Amsterdam quickly became a thriving center of trade, drawing a wide variety of ethnic stock to its muddy streets. The Dutch believed in tolerance, both in religion and of people whose skin might be a different color, and thus was born the melting pot which became New York City."

"Interesting," Chris commented.

"As much of the population at any given time was sailors, New Amsterdam could be a rowdy place, known for drink, prostitutes and brawls. The Dutch West Indies Company decided a firm hand was needed to keep the population in line, and so sent what was to be the last Dutch Director General of the settlement, Governor Peter Stuyvesant." Linda paused for an instant. "You mentioned Peter Stuyvesant in your story."

"That's correct," Chris nodded.

"Peter rolled into town on May 11, 1647, to a generally icy reception from the citizens of New Amsterdam, and he never really warmed to the place. Nor did it warm to him, despite many improvements he accomplished, such as the erection of the city wall, on the site of what became Wall Street, and the digging of a canal which eventually became Broadway. To some extent he was able to get the drinking and other vices in order by wielding an iron fist. Stuyvesant also clamped down on religious tolerance, which didn't do much to help with his popularity. He also fought, and lost the fight to keep the Jewish population of New Amsterdam from growing larger."

"Antisemitism, even back then," Chris snickered.

"That's right," Linda concurred. "Grim old Peter Stuyvesant had little respect or sympathy for the popular pastimes or social failings of his countrymen. He enacted ordinances to crack down on disturbances to the public order, such as firing of guns, beating of drums, and sale of liquor. Stuyvesant realized that he needed some type of municipal force to maintain order and enforce his ordinances. On August 12, 1658, a "Rattle-Watch" was formed, becoming one of the first public police forces in America."

"That's right," Chris nodded. "I have a memory of this Rattle Watch even though I have no idea what it really is."

"The rattle watchmen patrolled what is now New York City, using wooden rattles to warn people of threats or fires. The patrols carried green lanterns at night from sunset until dawn. When the lawmen returned, they hung their lanterns on a hook by the front door of the watch house to show they were on the job. Today, green lights are still placed outside the entrances of New York City police precincts as a symbol that the 'watch' is present and vigilant. The Rattle Watch was a combination of police officer, firefighter & hourly time caller who carried the equivalent of a wood New Year's Eve noisemaker that made a clacking racket."

"Yeah, yeah," Chris gushed. "It's good you can fill in the holes for me."

"Okay, Chris," Linda stated, "tell me your story."

Chris took a deep breath. "For as long as I can remember, I have only wanted to be one thing – a police officer."

"Does law enforcement run in your family."

"That's just it." Chris replied. "No one in my family has ever been a cop and I didn't have any friends who wanted to be cops."

"So," Linda added. "You don't know where your mysterious allure to law enforcement came from."

"Not a clue," Chris responded.

Chris went on to relate the story of all his past memories. Linda listened intently and provided commentary and historical perspective to his tale. At one point, Linda cut in. "Remember, Chris, in 1692 New Yorkers were very different from New Englanders. The world of wonders in which seventeenth-century New Englanders lived was a place where the boundary between the visible and invisible worlds was permeable, the war between God and the devil intense, and the influence of invisible powers—whether of the stars and planets or demons and spirits—was pervasive. Such beliefs were not just common among ordinary folk, they were shared by the learned. New York did not possess this puritanical belief in the supernatural that was rampant in their northern neighbors. While the hysteria of the Salem Witch Trials gripped New England, New York was mostly free of accusations of witchcraft. Still, New York was subject to English law and English law did recognize the criminality of witchcraft, much to the lament of your Katherine Harris."

During Chris's memories of the Andersons Linda provided additional clarification. "When you mentioned your memories of the Anderson's you said that Martha Anderson stopped at a broadside. Do you know what a broadside is?"

"Not a clue," Chris grinned.

"The broadside was usually located just outside the market and would be the first stop for people visiting the market area. Ever since Gutenberg invented his printing press in 1454 there had been broadsides. These notices, written on disposable single sheets of paper printed on one side only were posted prominently in the community to keep the citizens abreast of the latest news and much more: government proclamations, public service announcements, opinion papers, advertisements, and entertainment updates. Being a woman who could read, Martha Anderson would have been proud to stand in front of the broadside."

Linda also stopped Chris when he began speaking about farmer George McFarland. "During the middle decades of the eighteenth century there was ample opportunity for colonists in New York City. Jobs such as printers, clockmakers, barbers, tanners, milliners, dyers, and menders were in demand. With the constant activity in New York Harbor, the shipping industry was also booming. The largest industry in the City was agriculture, with farms peppering the northern landscape producing squash, beans, corn, melons, grapes, apples, peaches, flax, rye, wheat, and tobacco. So, it is not unusual that Mr. McFarland would have a very productive farm during that period."

When Chris talked about his memories of the wedding of George McFarland's daughter, Clara, to John Forsythe, Linda again added context to the story. "Just as today, a wedding was one of the most monumental moments in a person's life and were always highly anticipated and joyous events. Today's weddings can take place in any imaginable location – a church, dedicated wedding venue, cruise ship, beach resort, park, city hall, and on and on – but, in the 1700s, the large distances people often lived from an actual church building meant that the vast majority of weddings occurred at the brides' home, in this case, George McFarland's home."

When Chris related his memory of constable John Anderson dying in a Manhattan fire on the night of the wedding, Linda again added perspective. "That fire marked the beginning of what became known as the Conspiracy of 1741, a purported plot by slaves and poor whites to revolt and level New York City with a series of fires. Historians disagree as to whether such a plot existed, but according to your memory there was no question that Constable Anderson was dead."

When Chris finished his entire story, Linda took a sip of water and hesitated for a moment before speaking. "Your story is amazing, Chris. I have to begin by explaining to you that I am a skeptic."

Chris frowned. "So, you think I'm full of shit," he grumbled.

"Oh, no!" Linda reached across the table and grabbed his hand. "That's not what a skeptic is. With the subject of witchcraft, I simply look for explanations for events that are more reasonable that attributing the events to spells, magic, or curses. I don't know what happened to you, but I would certainly like to help you find out."

"Okay," Chris replied. "How are you going to help me?"

Linda ran her hand through her hair. "You told me the story of all your past memories, but can you tell me some specifics."

"I don't understand what you mean?" Chris replied.

"You've painted some broad strokes. Tell me some of the fine details you remember about day to day life from any of these people you remember."

"How long do you have?" Chris laughed. He touched his head. "There's a lot jammed in there. That's why I'm here. I could probably go on for days."

"Try telling me something you remember about one of these lives that you know happened, but you don't understand."

Chris sat back in his chair and took a deep breath. "Hmm, let me see. I remember that Baltis Van Steyer had four children – two boys and two girls. He always kept a coin next to each child's bed."

"Why did he do that?"

"Damned if I know," Chris shrugged.

"What else?"

Chris chuckled. "I also recall that Baltis would stick his kid's feet in the first snow of the winter."

"I guess he was playing with his kids," Linda said.

"No," Chris waved his hand. "It wasn't playing. It was something different. Some duty that he felt he had to do."

"Interesting," Linda remarked. "What else?"

"Thomas Anderson always carried a lucky charm with him."

"Many people carry lucky charms," Linda replied. "What did he carry?"

"A bone."

"Can you describe the bone?"

Chris nodded. "It was a codfish bone, three-quarters of an inch, narrow, notched, and pearly white." Chris raised his hand. "On second thought, he carried two bones – both from the head of the same fish."

"Anything else, Chris?"

He snickered. "I remember that Anderson's wife would have fit whenever he put bread down on the table a certain way."

"How was that?"

"She would go crazy whenever he would place buttered bread down with the buttered side down."

Chris went on for over an hour with specific details from these past lives. Linda finally brought the interview to a conclusion. "This has been an amazing experience for me. I want to thank you, Chris."

"Are you still a skeptic, Linda?"

"I will always be a skeptic, Chris."

"So, you do think I'm full of shit."

She shook her head. "I didn't say that. To the contrary. Something very extraordinary happened to you. Let me do a little research before I make any conclusions."

"Of course," Chris nodded. "But please remember – the moment they terminate me from the NYPD – I die!"

Linda opened her mouth but could not think of a good response to Chris's statement. She stood and extended her hand. "It was a pleasure meeting you, Chris, and I know I'll be talking to you again soon."

"I sure hope so," Chris mumbled.

•••

When Kyra entered the apartment, there was a repeat performance from the night before, except this time it was Kyra leading Linda into the bedroom with Linda bubbling with excitement over meeting Chris.

Kyra rolled over and cupped her hands around Linda's cheeks. "Sorry to stop you from briefing me on your interview, but there are priorities, you know."

Linda laughed as she extended her neck forward for a long, soulful kiss. "That's okay. How can I ever resist you?"

Kyra turned on her back. "So, what did you think of Chris?"

"Well, I left the asylum," Linda playfully punched Kyra's arm lightly, "thinking that I had heard an amazing story. Now, however, after I had the afternoon to do some research I have to say that this is an absolutely incredible story."

"This doesn't sound like my favorite little skeptic," Kyra giggled.

"It was all in the details," Linda said. "For over an hour I probed his story for small, specific details about the lives he has memories of."

"And?"

"And, he supplied detail after detail of incredible information."

"Like what?"

"Okay," Linda began. "He didn't know why, but he told me that Baltis Van Steyer always kept a coin next to the beds of his children."

"So?"

"So, in the 17th century a coin near a child's bed was thought to be a way to protect them from nose-bleeds."

"He could have looked that up," Kyra scoffed.

"There's much more," Linda continued. "He said Baltis would always stick his kid's feet in the first snow of the winter."

"Big deal. He was a father who enjoyed playing with his kids."

"That's what I thought," Linda said. "But Chris said it wasn't play – that there was some reason he had to do it."

"What reason?"

"I found out that some 17th century parents placed their children's feet in the snow to stave off croup."

"That's interesting."

"It gets better," Linda continued. "Chris remembered that the guy named Anderson from the early 18th century used to carry a bone for good luck."

Kyra sighed. "That's not such an incredible revelation."

"Oh no," Linda shot back. "He described the bone as being from a codfish head, three-quarters of an inch, narrow, notched, and pearly white."

"I guess that is incredible," Kyra admitted.

"There's more," Linda continued. "Chris remembered that Anderson actually carried two bones, and that both were from the head of the same codfish. I found an old colonial record that said some people carried this bone and that it was considered doubly good luck to have the second bone from the same head."

"Is there more?" Kyra asked.

Linda nodded her head. "He went on and on. I had to stop him. One of his revelations really got to me."

"What was it?"

"He said that Anderson's wife would get crazy angry at him whenever he would place buttered bread down with the buttered side down."

"That's crazy," Kyra responded. "I never heard of that superstition."

"Neither did I," Linda agreed. "But I dug deep and found that there was a small splinter group of the Anglican church that existed only in New York City in the early 18th century. This group had some very strange beliefs and superstitions, one of which was the belief that it was very bad luck to place buttered bread down with the buttered side down."

"Oh my God!" Kyra blurted. "That's eerie."

"I know," Linda concurred.

"So, you do believe in this curse, don't you?" Kyra gasped.

"Let's not go crazy," Linda cautioned. "I am still very much a skeptic, but I can't explain what happened to Chris and you have no psychiatric medical explanation, right."

"That's correct."

Linda bit her lip. "All I know is that if this kid gets fired from the NYPD and gets killed, I won't be able to live with myself."

"So, what should we do?" Kyra asked.

"We need professional advice." Kyra replied.

"Where will be find an expert?"

"Where else," Linda smiled. "At the witchcraft store."

CHAPTER 3: PROFESSIONAL WITCHES

November 21st: The bell attached to the inside of the door announced the presence of the visitors. The Sorcerer's Cauldron, the oldest witchcraft store in New York City, had not been open for an hour but already it was buzzing. Shoppers browsed in every aisle. A middle-aged man in a neat blue dress shirt, cellphone clipped to his belt was in the back of the shop, talking to one of the employees who carved custom candles for spells. Kyra heard him explain that he needed luck to close a business deal and that the deal could fall apart even after a contract was signed, so the spell had to last. The employee – perched on a stool under a sign that read "The Witch Is In" – started to carve intricate symbols into a huge pillar candle for the businessman.

"Good to see you professor." Shop owner Sandy Woods entered in a whirlwind, breaking the focus on the businessman. Sandy was a slender energetic woman, her arms and chest covered in intricate tattoos of pentagrams and ravens, her vibrant pink hair covered in a black bandanna. Her arms were full of plants for the shop's back garden, where ritual sabbaths, open to the community, were held eight times a year.

After 14 years in business in the East Village, with the rising rents of gentrification claiming so many small businesses, the Sorcerer's Cauldron's survival might make anyone believe in magic.

"It's good to see you too, Sandy. It's been a long time since we did undergrad together."

Sandy took a deep breath. "Too long. Even a witch can't control the passage of time."

Linda grabbed Kyra's hand. "This is Kyra."

"Nice to meet you Kyra." Sandy smiled. "I'd shake your hand but my hands are rather full right now."

Kyra shook her head. "That's okay. It's nice to meet you too, Sandy."

"Wow," Linda commented. "I didn't know witchcraft was such a good business. You've been open less than an hour and the joint is jumping."

Sandy put the plants on the front counter. "I can't complain." She pointed to the employee working on the businessman's lucky candles. "The carved candles are the shop's specialty and bestselling item, but we also offer a fully stocked apothecary with everything from mugwort to rosehips, an entire binder of custom oils and incense and a large selection of books." She pointed to the glass case in front of the cash register. "We also have the usual standards - a variety of tarot cards and silver occult jewelry, a shelf of statuettes of gods and goddesses."

Sandy led Linda and Kyra into a quiet backroom filled with the heavy smell of incense. "It's kinda spooky back here," Kyra remarked. "Is this where you perform spells?"

"The shop does not perform spells," Sandy replied. "We provide supplies that people use to perform a spell."

"Oh," Kyra chuckled. "You provide the supplies for other witches to perform black magic."

Sandy shook her head and frowned. "We strictly sell supplies for good magic, which is one reason we've been successful. The shop puts out positive energy, so positive energy comes back to it."

"I'm sorry," Kyra replied. "I didn't mean to offend you."

"None taken," Sandy shrugged. She pointed to the shelves on all the walls. "This is basically our stock room. Our bestsellers are uncrossing candles, candles that have been specially carved to remove a block in luck or life, to help people get unstuck when things are not going right. The candles, which in addition to uncrossing can be carved for everything from love to money, sell briskly. Books on the occult are the second bestselling item," Sandy reported with a smile. "I'm glad that in the modern age of ebooks people still like to read a physical book."

"Who is your typical customer?" Linda asked.

"Customers cut across genders, ages and professions," Sandy responded. "We get doctors, lawyers, bartenders, people who have been practicing pagans for 20 years and people who have never done any of this before in their life. Part of the popularity of witchcraft comes from people looking for a spiritual practice that gives them a measure of control."

Sandy pointed to two folding chairs resting against the wall. "Well, I know you told me on the phone there was a reason you wanted to talk to me so why don't you ladies grab chairs."

Sandy leaned back in her chair, stretched her arms and yawned. "That is quite a story," she nodded.

"Is there anything you can do about this curse or hex?" Linda asked.

"How would I know?" Sandy shrugged.

"Well, you are a witch, aren't you?" Linda shot back.

"Yeah, I'm a witch," Sandy nodded. "An entrepreneurial witch – a business witch."

"What does that mean?" Kyra asked.

Sandy sighed deeply. "Let me put it to you ladies this way. Do you like Broadway plays?"

"Sure," Linda nodded.

"So do I," Sandy agreed. "So do millions of other people."

Linda squinted and tilted her head slightly. "I don't think I see your point."

"Many people know everything there is to know about Broadway, but very few have the gift to actually make it to the stage." Sandy placed her hand on top of Linda's "You are one of the most well-versed people I know on the subject of witchcraft, as am I – but we don't have the gift."

"The gift?" Kyra questioned.

"That's right," Sandy nodded. "We don't have it."

"So, witchcraft is all bullshit," Kyra frowned.

Sandy waved her hand in front of her body. "That's not what I'm saying. Trust me, I've seen things that convince me one hundred percent that witchcraft is very real. All I am saying is that very few people really have the gift."

"So, who buys all this stuff in your store?" Kyra inquired.

"Mostly people like that businessman outside. People who read a book or watched a TV show and think they know what they are doing." Sandy smiled. "Thank God for these types or I would be out of business."

Linda curled her lip. "So, I guess the bottom line is that you can't help us."

"Sorry," Sandy shrugged.

Kyra looked to Linda. "This was a waste of time."

"I said I couldn't do anything myself," Sandy cut in. "I didn't say I couldn't help you."

Kyra laughed. "What is this, a witch riddle?"

Linda kicked Kyra under the table. "Be nice!"

"That's okay," Sandy replied. "I'd probably respond the same way if I were in your situation."

"How can you help us?" Linda asked.

"In all my years running this store and the thousands of customers I've dealt with, I've only met one person who truly has the gift." Sandy placed a hand on both of her visitor's hands. "You need to talk to Serena Duval."

November 22ⁿᵈ: The front door opened and the conversation commenced immediately "I'm having trouble not listening to your thoughts."

Kyra and Linda looked at each other wide eyed while Serena Duval continued. "Sorry, I kind of read into your heads a little bit."

Serena Duval was a plump aging woman. She was not overly old, but her body had aged passed her years so much so that she wore the wizened features of an old witch. The occasional strand of her once golden hair could still be seen though the lifeless grey mane that limply framed her aging face. Her forehead was wrinkled by many peaks and trenches - caused by years of consistent scowling - which unflatteringly crowned eyes that permanently harbored a disdainful glare, shadowing their beautifully unique shade of blue. Her entire face seemed drained of any signs of joy and amusement, instead her frumpy cheeks told a tale of regular displeasure. There was also a complicated look to Serena Duval. On one hand she looked like she just came off the set of the Wizard of Oz, but there was also a corporate look about her, the type of look you would find in a Manhattan real estate agent selling high end East Side condominiums.

The three women settled into a sofa in the living room. Serena was drinking a homemade "grounding" tea in her Victorian home in Jersey City under a dream catcher and within sight of what appeared to be a human skull. Kyra looked around to take in the scene. She was surrounded by nearly one hundred houseplants, the earthy smell of incense, and, according to Duval, several of Kyra's ancestral spirit guides, who had followed her in.

"You actually have a nun," Duval informed Kyra. "I don't know where she comes from, and I'm not going to ask her."

Kyra simply shrugged, unsure of how to respond to the revelation while Serena Duval went on with her introduction. She described herself as a seer capable of reading auras and connecting with "the other side"; a plant whisperer who communicated with her succulents; and one in a long line of healers in her family, which traced its roots to Cuba and the indigenous Taíno people[1], who settled in parts of the Caribbean. She was also a professional witch, selling anointing oils and "intention infused" body products in her online store. Serena also made a pitch for her main business – her online witchcraft school that she claimed had in excess of 900 students enrolled.

"What would I get out of your curriculum?" Kyra asked.

Serena smiled. "When you graduate, you feel magical."

Serena searched through a pile of papers and magazines on the coffee table, apparently not through with her self-promotion efforts. She pulled a magazine from the stack. "See," she said. "I was named Witch of the Year by Spirit Walkers magazine."

"Very impressive," Linda nodded. She looked at Kyra. "I think we should be going."

"Going?" Serena gasped. "Why would you go when you haven't accomplished your purpose?"

Linda snickered. "And I suppose you know our purpose because you read my thoughts."

Serena shook her head. "No, I know your purpose because I spoke with Sandy and she told me your story."

There was a moment of uncomfortable silence before Serena continued. "Look, I'm 60-years old and where I grew up my family's spell work was taboo. I had my first vision at age five. I grew up on food stamps, was homeless for parts of college, and, as an adult, sometimes skipped lunch to save up for rent." She swept her hand to all corners of her home. "The commercial success of witchcraft has manifested an entirely new life for me, and I don't apologize for it. It is not my fault that over the past decade, witchcraft, long viewed with suspicion and even hostility, has transmuted into a mainstream phenomenon."

---

1.   https://webcache.googleusercontent.com/

search?q=cache:u_nXXM0Sh_sJ:https://www.nationalgeographic.com/history/2019/10/meet-survivors-taino-tribe-paper-genocide/+&cd=2&hl=en&ct=clnk&gl=us

Serena smiled. "Casting spells and assembling altars have become quite lucrative."

"Why the resurgence in the interest in witchcraft?" Kyra asked.

"This latest witch renaissance coincides with a growing fascination with astrology, crystals, and tarot, which, like magic, practitioners consider ways to tap into unseen, unconventional sources of power—and which can be especially appealing for people who feel disenfranchised or who have grown weary of trying to enact change by working within the system. The more frustrated people get, they do often turn to witchcraft, because they're like, 'Well, the usual channels are just not working, so let's see what else is out there.' "

"So, how can you help us?" Linda asked.

"I live by two rules," Serena said as she ripped frankincense oil onto a candle on the coffee table. "First, I don't loan money out, and second, I always get paid up front for my services. You need a hex removed, right?"

"A curse," Linda corrected.

Serena waved her hand dismissively. "You call it a curse, I call it a hex – I use the proper terminology."

"You can do it?" Kyra remarked.

"I could take your money, light some candles, wave my arms and say the hex is broken, but that wouldn't be honorable."

"How can you help us?" Linda repeated.

"I can't break the hex, but I can tell you how it can be broken."

Linda raised her eyebrows. "Well?"

Serena smiled. "First, we have to deal with my second rule. It will be $250 for the information."

Kyra looked at Linda and sighed. "We don't have that much cash with us."

"That's okay," Serena replied. "I accept all major credit cards and Paypal."

Kyra looked at Linda. "You have your Amex card on you, right?"

With the transaction complete, Serena got down to business. "Sorry if this scares you, but hexes, cast to inflict misfortune on others, are indeed real, they've just been watered down over the years."

"What does that mean?" Kyra asked.

"It means that in recent years, fake witches – usually hipsters – have been hexing everything from Wall Street to Supreme Court Judge Brett Kavanaugh, to President Trump. Even though these phony hexes have no real-world impact, the practice has captured the hearts, and now the attention of the world."

"What about these so-called real hexes," Linda commented. "that's our concern."

"Have you ever heard of the rule of threes?" Serena asked.

Kyra and Linda shook their heads.

"It's the belief that performing magic with ill intent will come back to you three times, turning the ill intent on you. But the rule of threes doesn't simply mean, for example, that if you cast a spell to steal someone's man and you and said man get together, he'll cheat on you exactly three times. Hexes like this usually entail bigger blowback."

Kyra extended her arms to the side. "Then why would anyone place a hex if it was going to come back worse on them?"

"It's kind of like the checks and balances of the witch community," Serena explained. "I would never think about a hex because I know the repercussions to me."

"So, how does a hex ever get started?" Kyra asked.

"If a witch performs magic to cause harm to someone, she's probably in a pretty nasty, dark place. And in your story, that witch in 1692 was minutes from the gallows, so that's about as dark as it gets. She certainly was not worried about any repercussions to herself."

"So, how do we break the hex?" Linda asked.

"This is a lineage hex. It attaches itself to a line and remains there."

"Forever?" Kyra gasped.

Serena shook her head. "No, for as long as a direct descendent of the witch who cast the hex lives."

"So, when the line of direct descendants is broken, so is the hex?" Linda asked.

"Correct," Serna nodded.

"But there could be hundreds of direct descendants in the world", Linda agonized. "If that's the case this curse could go on forever."

"It's a hex – not a curse," Serena corrected. "It is true that the end of the line of direct descendants ends the hex, but a direct descendant can also remove the hex."

"How do we find a direct descendent?" Kyra asked.

Serena shrugged. "I'm a witch, not a genealogist."

Linda grabbed Kyra's arm. "Mike Whitten works with me at Columbia. He's done genealogy research for several people in my department – traced their families all the way back to the colonies. I'll talk to him."

"You could also reach out to the Sons of Massapequa," Serena suggested.

"Massapequa?" Kyra blurted. "The Long Island town?"

"The Sons of Massapequa is one of the oldest societies in North America. It traces its origins back to the original settlement in 1658. Before the Dutch settlers, the Massapequa Native American tribe lived in the area. The Massapequas were part of the Algonquin speaking people who made up the larger Lenape people who became known as the 13 tribes of Long Island. When the Dutch arrived in Massapequa the local tribe chief was Chief Tackapausha. Tackapausha and the Massapequas were said to be well-practiced in the magical arts, and they mixed well with a coven of witches among the original Dutch settlers."

Linda shook her head. "I'm sorry, Serena, but you lost me. How can the Sons of Massapequa help us break this hex?"

"It is rumored that the society were conscientious record keepers, and that they still have all their records from the 17th century, including names and information on the hexes."

"Wow!" Kyra looked at Linda. "I guess we'll be paying a visit to the Sons of Massapequa."

Serena held up her right hand in the universal sign for stop. "Proceed down that path with due caution."

"What does that mean?" Kyra asked.

"I'd be surprised if they talked to you. They tend to be very tight lipped about their organization."

"Then why should we waste out time visiting them," Linda laughed.

"Because of reality," Serena replied.

"Again, you've lost me," Kyra chuckled.

Serena took a deep breath. "The reality is that the Sons of Massapequa are dying. Their membership is way down across the country, so maybe it would be in their best interest to start opening up a bit."

CHAPTER 4: THE CLOCK IS TICKING

November 25th: The serenity of a few days earlier had turned out to be a total anomaly. Kyra had been on duty for three hours and hadn't stopped to take a breath. It was one emergency after the other with the patients and their problems overlapping each other. Kyra chuckled to herself when she considered that this was insanity taking place in a psychological emergency room. Kyra collapsed against the wall while two security guards wrestled with her latest emergency. She needed some excuse for a break – anything to give her a chance to collect her thoughts.

It was Kristin Clark's voice from the nurse's station shouting over the chaos that provided the opportunity. "Dr. Thomas, there's a call for you on line two. He says it's urgent."

Kyra didn't care if it was a telemarketer on the line – she was taking the call. "Thanks Kris," she blurted as she hustled past the desk. "I'll take it in the doctor's lounge."

Kyra flipped on the light in the empty lounge and let out a huge exhale as she collapsed in the soft chair. She wanted to close her eyes, but she noticed the flashing light on the phone next to the chair.

"Dr. Thomas, may I help you?"

"It's Chris Bennington, Dr. Thomas."

"Chris," Kyra gushed. "I'm glad you called. I'll bet your happy to be home."

"Yeah, I'm very happy to be home," Chris sighed.

Kyra noted Chris's somber tone. "That's funny, you don't sound very happy. What's wrong Chris?"

"I had to appear at the NYPD's Medical Division today."

"What happened?" Kyra asked.

"They told me that since there is no physical reason for my seizure, I would be a risk to put on patrol, so they are surveying me off the job."

"You're be fired?" Kyra gasped.

"No," Chris replied. "I'm being given a half pay medical disability pension."

"Well, I guess that's not the end of the world."

"It is for me," Chris groaned. "It really doesn't matter if I get fired, or if they give me a pension, the result will still be the same – I'm dead!"

"I don't necessarily think you're dead," Kyra commented.

"I thought you believed me," Chris quipped. "I guess I was wrong."

"Wait a minute, Chris," Kyra tried to right the ship. "I never said I didn't believe you. In these past few days I've seen and heard a lot of strange things. All I am saying is that I'm hoping we can still work out a good outcome for you."

"How are you gonna do that?" Chris grumbled.

"How long until the police department separates you from the department?"

"They didn't say."

"Well," Kyra took a deep breath. "I was your attending physician in the ER. They are going to need my report before they can take any action."

"So, I get a temporary reprieve," Chris groaned. "Big deal! I get to be a rubber gun for a while."

"A rubber what?"

"The rubber gun squad," Chris clarified. "When cops get their guns taken away for disciplinary, medical or psychological reasons, they dump them in non-enforcement assignments like working at the auto pound or being part of the barrier unit."

"What is the barrier unit?" Kyra asked.

"Those are the cops that put up the police barricades. They work out of Queens and every day they load up a flatbed truck with the newer metal and older wooden police barriers and drop them off at the sites of parades, demonstrations and other public gatherings."

"They don't really give them rubber guns, do they?"

"No," Chris laughed. "It's just an expression for a cop who has had his gun removed."

Kyra felt better at hearing Chris laugh. "Don't be so negative," she directed. "It gives us some time to find a solution. But the first thing I need to do is talk to the Medical Division people at the NYPD."

. . .

November 26th: In the predawn hour, the drive on the Long Island Expressway from Long Island City took only ten minutes. Named for its developer, Samuel J. Lefrak, Lefrak City was a very large apartment development in the southernmost region of Corona and the easternmost part of Elmhurst, a neighborhood in the New York City borough of Queens. The complex of twenty 17-story apartment towers covered 40 acres and housed over 14,000 people in 4,605 apartments. The site included sitting and play areas, sports courts, a swimming pool, a branch of the Queens Borough Public Library, a post office, two large office buildings, shops, and over 3,500 parking spaces. Nestled away in the upper floors of one of the office buildings was the NYPD Medical Division.

At 6 AM Kyra was able to secure a legal parking space in front of the building, but she still slid the MEDICAL DOCTOR ON CALL parking placard onto her dashboard, for whatever good it may do.

When Kyra emerged from the elevator she immediately assessed the cop seated at the reception desk. *This must be a rubber gun squad cop,* she thought. To sit at a desk at the entrance to the Medical Division would not seem to be an enforcement assignment. Kyra envisioned Chris sitting at the same desk before long.

This baby-faced cop could not have been much more than 25-years of age. He appeared to have been in a pitched battle to stay awake on his post, but the sight of the approaching visitor shocked him to life. "I have an appointment to see Lieutenant Evans."

"Just sign the log and go right in ma'am." The cop easily returned to his state of semi-consciousness.

Kyra signed the log and headed for the door.

The silence of the waiting room seemed complete, bereft of any noise or rustling as Kyra stared at some unknown entity on the floor.

The hurried footsteps and squeak of the door broke the silence. "Good morning, Doctor Thomas, I'm Lieutenant Evans."

Mike Evans was short and stocky with pattern baldness found in many forty-five-year old males. He wore a rumpled white dress shirt with an open top button with an untied red tie hanging over both shoulders. Kyra felt bad that she was bothering the lieutenant after he had worked all night, and she was a bit shocked when he mentioned that he had just arrived five minutes earlier.

"Dr. Morgan is one of our supervising psychiatrists," the lieutenant stated. "I figured we would discuss this matter in his office."

Doctor Nigel Morgan was a black man in his late 40's. When he extended his hand and provided a pleasant greeting Kyra could hear the Caribbean lilt to his voice. His suit was somewhat shabbier than Kyra expected for someone of his position, but then maybe that was deliberate. She figured that he did not want to put his police patients off by being too showy. As Kyra told the story of Chris Bennington, Dr. Morgan glanced at his paperwork, scribbled notes. occasionally glancing up at Kyra with a question or comment. Kyra wondered if the lack of eye contact was deliberate and was supposed to put her at ease, and make her feel less threatened in the intimating environment of the NYPD. If that was the intent, it was working. Kyra liked the whole package; the shabby suit, his manner and the run-down office. She admired that he must have some sort of calling to be here with these troubled police officers and not in some sort of swanky upscale place.

When Dr. Morgan perceived that Kyra was finished with her story, he dropped his pen on top of his notes and sat back in his chair, nodding his head slowly. "I have been a psychiatrist for 23-years, and I must admit that this is one of the more unique stories I have heard. And I can understand the interest you have taken in this case, especially in your role as the attending psychiatrist."

Kyra smiled. "I sense a 'but' coming, Dr. Morgan."

Dr. Morgan returned the smile. "You are very insightful, Dr. Thomas – but, the safety of the citizens is always the paramount issue in my decisions. You are prepared to say that Chris Bennington does not pose a threat to the citizenry and can function as a New York City police officer. That's fine – but I must account for the episode he experienced. You say he is not suffering from any psychosis, but there was no physical explanation found – no seizure, no epileptic event – nothing. So how do you explain the event as something other than a serious psychological trauma?" Dr. Morgan smiled. "Unless you are telling me that you believe he is being controlled by a spell cast by a witch in the 17th century."

Kyra looked down and shook her head. She had enough sense not to go down that road. "No, obviously, I'm not insinuating that Chris Bennington is cursed. I'm just saying that I do not see any medical or psychological reason that he can't perform his job."

"Until another episode occurs," Dr. Morgan remarked.

Lieutenant Evans joined the conversation, "Look, Dr. Thomas. We don't take these decisions lightly, but the safety of the citizens has to always be our top priority." He shook his head. "I'm sorry, but we just can't take the risk of putting Chris Bennington on patrol."

"So, you're going to fire him," Kyra remarked.

Evans held up his right hand. "I didn't say that. We understand that this is a unique case. Even though a probationary officer can be terminated for no reason, we are going to process Chris for an ordinary medical disability retirement where he will receive a half pay pension." The lieutenant shrugged. "I know it's not much – half of a recruit's salary, but at least it's something."

"When will this become effective?" Kyra asked.

Lieutenant Evans glanced at a calendar on the wall. "Let's see. His file will be complete as soon as we receive the final report from the attending." He turned to Kyra. "In other words, Dr, Thomas, as soon as we receive your final report."

"And I have 21-days from the time of the patient's discharge to complete my report," Kyra remarked.

"That's right," Lieutenant Evans nodded. "You have 21-days and then the Medical Division takes a couple of days to process the case." Evans smiled wryly. "Assuming you take the full 21-days, I would say that Chris Bennington's medical disability retirement should take effect on Monday, December 22nd."

In the car ride to the hospital, all Kyra could think of was December 22nd. If she truly believed this whole unlikely story, Chris Bennington would die at that time unless she could figure out some solution. As ridiculous as it seemed, the best and most immediate course of action seemed to be trying to track down a direct descendent of the witch who initiated the hex, and the most expeditious path to this information seemed to be through the Sons of Massapequa.

CHAPTER 5: THE SONS OF MASSAPEQUA

December 1st: The building on Hempstead Turnpike in the Long Island Village of Massapequa had been in disrepair for a generation. At least that's what the Pakistani attendant in the gas station convenience store told Kyra and Linda. The attendant could not verify the address or who owned the building or why it hadn't been either demolished or refurbished. Based on the addresses of the surrounding properties, Kyra and Linda concluded that the run-down building had to be their destination. It was a gaunt shell of a mansion. The windows were fancy mullioned sash types, but some were cracked and all the glass was grey with the grime of many years.

They approached via a very old, very cracked concrete walkway. The door was thick oak with a brass knocker that looked like a lion head. Kyra ignored the ornate knocker when Linda pointed to a button on the left side of the door frame. Kyra could hear the bell sounding on the inside of the door. It had a strangled sound, as though it's battery was somewhat drained. Linda winced as the door began to open, its creaking noise brought a chill to her spine. It sounded like some dying animal, crying out its pain and sorrow with its last breath.

The man on the other side of the door couldn't have been more than forty-five or so, but he walked with a cane. His right leg had the fluidity of youth but the other was jagged like he couldn't control it. Kyra had seen eighty- year old's walk better than that. From his complexion Kyra couldn't help but imagine him in Greece donning a fresh white shirt and sable shorts, but on this New York chilly day he was layered up for the temperature outside. His eyes scanned Kyra and Linda as he motioned for the ladies to enter. He raised his eyebrows in what Kyra hoped was a greeting as they entered the dimly lit foyer. He waved for Kyra and Linda to follow him into a private office where he labored to move behind a large oak desk. He gestured for his guests to sit before settling in his own chair with heavy awkwardness.

The walk from the foyer to behind the large desk seemed to have worn the man out. He propped his cane against the wall and took a few deep breaths. He then smiled towards his guests. "I'm George Goff. It's a pleasure to meet you ladies."

"It was nice of you to meet with us on such short notice," Linda said.

George shrugged. "I'll do what I can to help you. You said on the phone you were interested in learning about my organization."

"Yes," Kyra nodded.

George leaned back in his chair. "The Sons of Massapequa is North America's oldest fraternal organization. Despite its longevity, the Sons have long been shrouded in mystery. To outside observers, our rites and practices may seem cult-like, clannish and secretive — even sinister. Some of this stems from the Sons often deliberate reluctance to speak about the organization to outsiders."

"But you agreed to talk to us," Linda remarked.

"That's right," George nodded. "You see, the Sons of Massapequa is a worldwide organization with a long and complex history. Its members have included politicians, engineers, scientists, writers, inventors and philosophers. Many of these members have played prominent roles in world events, such as revolutions, wars and intellectual movements.

"The name of your organization might be considered sexist, right?" Kyra jabbed.

George chuckled. "As the name implies, a fraternal organization is one that's composed almost solely of men who gather together for mutual benefit, frequently for professional or business reasons. However, nowadays women can be Sons."

"So, what exactly is the purpose of the Sons of Massapequa?" Linda asked.

"We are bound together by secret rites of initiation and ritual. Our members ostensibly promote the brotherhood of man, and in the past, have often been associated with 17th century harmony of mind and spirit as found by the Dutch settlers in the Massapequa Native American tribe. This is not to say that the Sons are wholly secular and devoid of religious aspects, we just are more inclusive and open minded."

"How did the Dutch become involved with the Massapequa tribe?" Kyra asked.

"Our Grand Chief is Tackapausha, the chief of the Massapequa tribe when the Dutch arrived. Tackapausha introduced the Dutch to a special form of spirituality that exists in the Sons to this day. While many of the Sons are Christians, the Sons of Massapequa and Christianity have had a complex, often divisive, relationship. Some orthodox Christians have taken issue with the Sons form of spirituality and its frequently perceived ties to paganism and the occult. But the Catholic Church has been among its harshest critics. In 1762, a Papal decree prohibited Catholics from becoming Sons. Even today, the Papal ban on the Sons of Massapequa remains in place, with the Church declaring the Sons irreconcilable with the doctrine of the Church."

"Could it be that those original settlers and the Massapequa tribe were involved with witchcraft?" Linda probed.

George shrugged. "The origins of the Sons of Massapequa are obscure, and the subject is rife with myth and speculation. One of the more fanciful claims is that the Sons formed after Tackapausha cast a spell to give a fatal disease to a neighboring tribe that was threatening the Dutch and Massapequas."

Linda curled her lip. "For some reason I'm getting the feeling you are not telling us everything."

George laughed. "There are no deep, dark secrets, but like many societies of that time, we have jealously guarded our secrets and were selective about who we chose for membership. Initiation for new members requires a long period of training, during which they learn what it is to be a true Son. Most early fraternal organizations were almost exclusively male, but women have always played an active role in our organization."

"So, you are a progressive secret society," Kyra mocked.

George did not react to the jibe. "Similar to our long relationship with women, the history of the Sons of Massapequa is one of inclusion with all racial and ethnic minorities. Remember, the Sons of Massapequa is not a local Long Island organization. We have chapters all over North America and several prominent historical figures have been Sons."

"Could we get back to the organization's association with witchcraft?" Linda asked.

"I'd love to," George replied, "but there is no association. The world of spirituality is composed of esoteric signs and symbols that are baffling to most people. Therefore, they find organizations like the Sons of Massapequa unsettling and perhaps a bit frightening, and words like witchcraft are thrown around easily. Such is the case with the organization's symbol of an eye in the moon. Although there is not a single, universally agreed upon meaning, even among members, most Sons contend that these two objects in conjunction are meant to represent the organization's principles – the all-seeing eye in the moon, a symbol of nature, mother, rebirth, and spirituality."

"It's sound like you are part of quite an organization," Linda remarked.

"I am," George agreed. "Unfortunately, the organization is declining in membership. The pull to join an exclusive, privileged enclave of enlightened people does not carry the attraction it once had. Although there are lodges in every U.S. state, many of these now stand vacant."

"Why is that?" Kyra asked.

"One of the reasons for this decline has been competition from similar fraternal and service organizations, such as the Odd Fellows, the Knights of Columbus, and the Benevolent and Protective Order of Elks. But it's also possible that this decline can be explained by the different values espoused by the newer generations, value systems that are often at odds with the previous generations." George shook his head. "The problem of decline is also rooted in the current composition of the lodges. I'm a kid," he laughed. "Most members are between the ages of 60 and 70. The Sons just don't seem to appeal to the younger generation."

George slapped his hands down on his desktop. "So, could I interest you ladies in applying to become Sons of Massapequa?"

Linda shook her head. "As appealing as it sounds, we actually came here for a different reason."

"What can I do for you?" George asked.

"We are very interested in your early history," Linda began. "There was a woman named Katherine Harris who was executed in New York City in 1692 for the charge of practicing witchcraft. We think this woman traces back to your organization and we have been told that you still keep written records from that time."

George's congenial manner had disappeared. "That's absurd – witchcraft records. That's the problem with society today. If you have any kind of a closed fraternal organization, people automatically assume you are casting spells and dancing around fires."

"So, you have no early records," Kyra probed.

"I'm sorry, ladies, I can't help you. And I would ask you to show yourselves out. I hope you can understand that it is something of an effort for me to get out from behind this desk."

"Thank you for your time," Kyra said.

"Yes, thank you," Linda concurred.

When the large entrance door creaked shut, George Goff labored to reach down to his belt. He tapped a few keys on his iPhone before placing the device to his ear. "It's George. I think we may have a problem."

"Well, that was a waste of time," Kyra moaned. "What do we do now?"

Linda activated the left signal and focused on her side view mirror as she eased into traffic on Hempstead Turnpike. "Let not your heart be troubled, my dear. We simply switch to plan B."

"Plan B?"

"Mike Whitten," Linda declared.

"Who's Mike Whitten?"

"You don't remember?" Linda lamented. "He's my friend from work who does the genealogy research."

"Well," Kyra grumbled. "You better get your friend on board quickly because our clock is counting down."

•••

December 2nd: The twelve men slowly ambled into the large meeting room. They were all as old and worn as the building on Hempstead Turnpike. The meeting room exemplified the disrepair displayed throughout the entire structure. The floor was covered by a stained commercial carpet that provided a musty odor to the entire room. The wooden tables and chairs were worn and scuffed and cracks covered the entire ceiling.

The entire wall in the front of the room was covered by an exquisite mural depicting the Massapequa Chief Tackapausha meeting with 17th century Dutch colonists. The numerous cracks in the wall took away from the appeal of the work of art, but it fit perfectly with the dilapidated condition of the entire facility.

George Goff limped to the front of the room with the assistance of his cane and sat at the desk in front of the mural. All the men sat silently on chairs facing the mural except for a man with a pale complexion and black sunken eyes who stood to Goff's right.

Goff pounded his cane on the desktop even though silence already filled the room. "I summoned you all here today to notify you of a potentially serious problem."

"What problem?" an old man sitting directly in front of Goff growled.

"There may be a threat to the society regarding the lineage hex."

There was still only silence in the room as Goff continued. "As you know, the last time the hex manifested itself was in 1996 when Police Officer Charles Johnson was sacrificed. The energy of the hex was passed to another named Christopher Bennington."

A gravelly voiced old man to Goff's left scoffed at Goff's warning. "Why have you inconvenienced us and sounded this baseless alarm.

66

Things are proceeding as they always have. Mr. Bennington will become a police officer and will eventually pay the required price."

"Mr. Bennington has become a police officer," Goff replied. "He was sworn in to the NYPD several days ago."

"There," the gravelly voice continued. "Things are as they should be. Mr. Bennington will have a fruitful career and when his time comes he will die for his oath."

"His time is here," Goff replied. "Bennington had a bad reaction to the acquisition of the memories and ended up in a mental ward."

"So?" the gravelly voice responded. "He will simply die sooner and pass on the hex."

"There may be complications," Goff remarked. "How do you think I know about Bennington's situation. I was visited by two women, one of who was the psychiatrist treating Bennington. They asked about our records to see if they could identify a direct descendant of Katherine Harris."

Grumbles and other sounds of shock and surprise arose from the audience. The gravelly voice had a question. "It has been so long since we had any issues, refresh my memory. What avenues would these women have in their quest?"

Goff took a deep breath. "There are currently two opportunities for them – one is in Los Angeles and the other is in Iceland."

Another man with a high-pitched voice joined the discussion. "So, there really isn't much chance of them being successful, is there?"

"Probably not," Goff replied. "But it is still a potentially serious situation, so I felt I had to brief all of you."

The gravelly voice returned. "So, now that you have told us about this potentially serious situation, what do you propose to do about it?"

Goff pointed to the silent man with the black sunken eyes standing next to him. "We will keep a close eye on the women to see if they make progress with their quest."

"Why take chances," the high-pitched voice chimed in. "why don't you eliminate the women?"

"Because we are not murderers," Goff sneered. "Don't worry though, there are other ways to handle the situation if they begin to get close."

CHAPTER 6: DESCENDANTS

December 14th: Kyra looked up at the sound of the key turning in the door. The person behind Linda was a young man, Asian, handsome as hell. He held his jacket in his hand revealing that he was clad in a tight black t-shirt and jeans, all as perfect as the day they were purchased. She could detect the scent of an exquisite cologne lingering in the air. She closed her eyes momentarily and leaned back in the sofa. The aroma was enough to flood her brain with endorphins, it was heady, perfect. She instinctively scanned his hands for a wedding ring - none. What was she doing? She had to remind herself that she wasn't attracted to men.

Kyra rose from the sofa as Linda approached with a peck on the lips. "Hey babe." She turned and extended her hand. "This is my good friend Mike Whitten."

Kyra moved forward and extended her hand. "It's a pleasure to meet you Mike. Thank you so much for helping us."

"It's alright," Mike shrugged. "I would do anything for my girl Linda. Besides, I love doing this research so it's not really work. It's more like enjoying a hobby."

"Well then," Kyra laughed. "Perhaps you should be thanking us for allowing you to enjoy your hobby."

"Let's not go crazy." Mike chuckled and held up both hands. "I love this stuff but Linda gave me a deadline of only a couple of weeks to come up with some information. Research like this usually takes me six months, so the time considerations did take a little of the fun out of it."

Kyra tilted her head. "I'm sorry."

"It's okay," Mike replied. "I'll live. But I won't live if I don't use your restroom very quickly."

"Of course," Linda said. She pointed to the left. "Down the hall."

Mike placed his briefcase on the polished wood floor and disappeared down the hallway.

"Wow!" Kyra gasped. "He is really good looking."

"Hey!" Linda grabbed Kyra around the waist. "Don't get any ideas," she laughed. "You're all mine."

"Don't worry," Kyra smiled as she leaned forward and kissed Linda. She pulled back and curled her lips. "But he is really handsome."

"I'll get you later," Linda warned as she playfully swatted Kyra's butt.

The distant sound of the flush preceded Mike's return. "Whew," he said. "Now I can function again."

Mike picked up his briefcase and scanned the apartment. "Where should I set up?"

"The dining room table, I guess," Linda shrugged.

Mike spread out several folders on the table. "Aside from the time constraints, this was still a very unique project for me."

"Why?" Kyra asked.

"It didn't occur to me until I began the research that this was going to be a first for me."

"How's that?" Linda questioned.

"I always work back. I have someone who wants their family tree traced so I start with the present day and work backward. This was the first time I was working forward. You gave me a name from 1692 as the starting point and I had to trace the family tree forward."

"Was that more difficult?" Kyra asked.

"It was still challenging, but actually, it was easier because the deeper I got into the tree the more records were available because I was moving forward in time. Usually, the deeper I get the records become more difficult to find."

"So," Linda rubbed her hands together. "What do you have for us, Mikey?"

Mike opened the folder directly in front of him. "The information you provided me was that Katherine Harris was found guilty of witchcraft in New York City in 1692 and executed."

"That's right," Kyra nodded.

"I got lucky right out of the box with records from the Supreme Court of Judicature."

"What's that?" Linda inquired.

"The Supreme Court of Judicature was established in 1691 and was succeeded by the present Supreme Court in 1847. The Supreme Court of Judicature was vested with unlimited original jurisdiction over all civil and criminal cases. However, the court rarely heard criminal cases after the Revolution, and it normally decided only the more important civil cases. But back in 1692 this court handled every big case in New York, especially cases with the death sentence. I found the record of Katherine Harris's case, but more importantly, the case record included her personal information including her next of kin."

Mike unrolled a large poster on the table. "So, with the main root of our tree being Katherine Harris we have three branches from her three children – Constance, Thomas, and Edward." Mike looked up from the poster. "Another advantage I had was that you were only interested in tracing direct descendants, so I could forget about all the branches that would develop from other relatives."

"Were you able to trace the three lines?" Linda asked.

Mike pointed to the middle line. "The line from Thomas Harris was easy. He died in 1698 from fever with no wife or children."

"That sucks," Linda commented. "I don't know what you're so upbeat about."

"All I said what that the line was easy to trace," Mike chuckled. "And it was easy. The line began and ended with Thomas Harris."

"Okay," Kyra jumped in. "Enough about poor Thomas. What about the other lines?"

Mike pointed to the line of the left. "The Constance Harris line was very solid and very easy to trace."

"That's great," Linda nodded.

"As a matter of fact," Mike continued. "When we reach the 20th century there are six identified direct descendants – Joseph Hanna, age

26. Edgar Stone, age 19, Paul Bello, age 29, Alan Frost, age 22, and his two brothers David Frost, age 21, and Peter Frost, age 24.

"Wait a minute," Linda quipped. "How do you have ages associated with all these guys?"

"Because that's how old they were when they died."

"What?" Kyra gasped.

"That's right," Mike nodded. "All six descendants from this line were killed in France in 1918 at the Battle of Saint Mihiel. And none of them had any children, so that line is dead."

"Well," Kyra moaned. "We're down to the Edward Harris line. Go ahead and give us the bad news."

"Bad news?" Mike grinned. "What bad news?" He placed his index finger on the name Edward Harris. "Edward Harris had three children."

"Wait!" Linda snapped. "With all due respect to your research methods, Michael, we can't handle the suspense. Please cut to the chase. Are there any direct descendants still alive?

"Yes," Mike replied.

"Yessss!" Kyra leaned over the table and exchanged a high five with Linda.

"But," Mike cautioned. "You may want to hear everything before you start celebrating."

"Uh oh," Kyra moaned.

"The first direct descendent is 64- year – old Gunnar Eglisson."

"That's a strange name," Kyra remarked.

Mike shook his head. "Not if you live in Akureyri, Iceland."

"He lives in Iceland?" Kyra wailed.

"What about descendant number two?" Linda asked.

Mike cleared his throat. "53-year old Michael Carlino from Los Angeles."

Linda deflated in her chair. "Los Angeles? It might as well be Iceland."

"Michael Carlino," Kyra repeated. "Why is that name familiar to me?"

"Did you ever watch the sitcom *Extra Cheese?*" Mike asked.

Kyra snapped her fingers. "That's it! He was the 'I can't wait till tomorrow because I get better looking every day' guy."

"Huh?" Linda squinted.

"You never watched Extra Cheese?" Kyra asked.

"I guess not," Linda shrugged "because I don't even know what it is."

"About twenty years ago," Kyra began, "It was a sitcom set in a fast food restaurant. Michael Carlino played one of the restaurant workers and he only had one line every episode. Whenever a customer would ask him how he was doing he would respond, "I can't wait till tomorrow because I get better looking every day."

"Sounds hilarious," Linda responded, rolling her eyes.

"It was so stupid it was funny," Kyra replied. "And it was on for a few seasons."

"Five seasons to be exact," Mike clarified.

Linda held up her hands. "Okay, enough with your journey through television history. How does identifying this washed up actor as a direct descendant help us? We have a week to get this guy here. Let's face it. There is no way this is going to happen."

Mike held up his hand and smiled. "Just put all the doom and gloom on hold for a minute. This is why you always get your money's worth with my research."

"What do you mean?" Linda asked.

"I did my due diligence on Mr. Michael Carlino. He has been divorced four times and has never had another television role since Extra Cheese."

"That's fascinating," Kyra mocked, "but how does that help us."

Mike ignored the jibe and continued. "Carlino makes his living now traveling the country on the autograph circuit. Every week he appears at some convention and signs autographs for a fee." Mike paused for a moment as he glanced back and forth between Kyra and Linda. "And this Saturday, the 21st, he will be appearing at TVcon at the Javitz Center in Manhattan."

"What the hell is TVcon?" Linda asked.

"It's one of those conventions, like ComicCon. With TVcon, a load of old television personalities sign autographs."

"Bear in mind," Kyra chimed in, "Sunday will be our zero hour. You think we are going to go to this washed up TV actor jamboree – meet this Carlino guy and convince him to come with us that night to help break a hex began by his great, great, great,great,great,great,great,great grandmother."

Mike smiled. "Do you have a better idea?"

"I have no idea," Kyra moaned.

"Kyra's right," Linda joined in. "This will never work."

"Hang on, ladies," Mike cautioned. "I have one more tidbit of information. Everything I read about Carlino said he is a real ladies man." Mike corrected himself. "Ladies man probably isn't the right word. Snake is probably a better description."

Linda shook her head. "You're losing me Michael."

"It's simple," he explained. "You go to the convention and wait on line for his autograph. When you get to the front of the line you come on to him like there is no tomorrow. You'll have no trouble hooking a snake like this. Just make sure you get there early so he won't have snared another date for the evening."

"You make it sound so simple," Kyra scoffed. "We're just going to walk up to this guy and say 'wow, you're so handsome and great. Please come have sex with me tonight.'"

Mike shrugged. "Something like that – but not both of you. That could scare him off. Kyra should go alone."

"Why Kyra?" Linda snarled.

"You're my girl," Mike crooned. "And you're beautiful. But Kyra is a few years younger and has a more exotic look, and that is just the type of look that Carlino is apparently drawn to."

"Okay," Linda nodded. "I'm starting to see a plan come together. We arrange a time and a place Saturday night to meet with Serena Duval for this de-hexing ceremony and then Kyra goes to TVcon that morning and tells Don Juan to meet her at the same location that night."

"That's the deal," Mike declared.

"Do you know how many things can go wrong with this plan?" Kyra fretted.

"I know," Linda agreed. "At least it's a chance. If we don't try it there's no chance."

•••

"Hi Serena, It's Linda Warren. We met a couple of weeks ago regarding removing the curse from the 17th century."

"You didn't have to tell me. I knew it was you calling – and it's a hex, not a curse."

Linda pulled the phone away from her ear and rolled her eyes. "Sorry. Well then Serena, do I need to tell you why I'm calling?"

"Probably not, but I don't want to do all of your work, so go ahead and tell me what you want."

Linda took a deep breath and composed herself. "Okay, Serena. We were able to locate a direct descendent of Katherine Harris."

"Who is Katherine Harris?"

Linda's mouth dropped wide open. "Katherine Harris – the witch in 1692 who was executed and placed a hex on police officers that is effecting one of Kyra's patients."

"Oh, of course I remember," Serena confirmed. "I was just distracted by one of my cats. So, my information about the Sons of Massapequa was helpful to you."

"Actually," Linda hesitated, "that information was a complete waste of time. The Sons of Massapequa were no help."

"Then how did you find a direct descendant?"

"Good, old fashioned family tree tracing."

"So why do you need me?" Serena asked.

"The clock is winding down for Kyra's patient. I'm still skeptical about this curse."

"Hex," Serena corrected.

"Sorry, hex," Linda said. "I keep forgetting the terminology. Anyway, Kyra's patient is going to be terminated from the police department on Monday, so if this curse...I mean hex is authentic, he should be killed in the line of duty just before the termination occurs.

Since we now have a direct descendant of Katherine Harris we want to remove the hex before then."

Serena's voice was devoid of any emotion. "One thousand dollars, payable in advance."

"One thousand dollars?" Linda gasped.

"It's non-negotiable," Serena replied. "Take it or leave it."

"Alright, alright," Linda groaned.

"Very good," Serena responded. "I can fit you in on Tuesday night the 23rd."

"Wait a minute," Linda blurted. "Have you not heard a word I said?"

"What?"

"The curse will get him by Monday."

"Hex," Serena corrected again.

"Whatever," Linda was out of patience. "We have to do this Saturday night."

"Sorry," Serena sighed, "but I'm already booked to do a moon ceremony in Central Park for a Manhattan coven. It's a regular gig and these ladies are my best customers."

"Couldn't you lift this hex and do your moon dance at the same time?" Linda suggested. "I would think your Manhattan witches would get a thrill out of lifting a hex to go along with howling at the moon – sort of like a bonus you offer."

"They don't howl at the moon," Serena scowled, "but you may be on to something. They might enjoy some variety to the moon ceremony."

"Excellent!" Linda declared.

"The coven and I will be in a clearing in the middle of a group of trees just inside the park at 66th Street and 5th Avenue at 9pm. You should get there a little later."

"Great!" Linda exclaimed. "So, we're all set?"

"As soon as I see a thousand dollars in my Paypal account," Serena clarified.

"It will be there," Linda groaned.

CHAPTER 7: THE CEREMONY

December 20th: "Chris!" Kyra sang. "It's good to hear your voice. How have you been?"

"I'm good, Dr. Thomas," Chris sighed.

"Wow!", Kyra snickered. "You sound like you are a ball of joy."

"Well, you know how it is doctor. My time is running out."

Kyra attempted to change the dynamic of the conversation. "Where did you end up being assigned?"

"The auto pound."

"Where's that?"

"Over by Kennedy Airport."

"What do you do there?"

"I'm assigned to intake. Whenever a vehicle comes into the pound, I inventory all the contents inside the vehicle and the trunk."

"Why do vehicles come to the auto pound?" Kyra asked.

"Various reasons," Chris replied. "Recovered stolen vehicles, derelict vehicles, vehicles seized for forfeiture."

"Sounds interesting," Kyra gushed.

"It's not," Chris grumbled. "And it really doesn't matter because in a few more days this will all be over." There was a momentary pause before Chris continued, his voice more upbeat. "It is good to hear from you, Dr. Thomas. I thought you forgot about me."

"Of course, I didn't forget about you, Chris." Kyra chuckled. "And even though we believe you are going to be fine, Professor Warren and I have been working on your situation."

"Really?" Chris replied. "What's happening with it?"

"For what it's worth," Kyra began. "We identified a direct descendant to the witch who placed the hex on Baltis Van Steyer."

"Why is that important?" Christ asked.

"According to our source, a direct descendant must be present to remove the hex. Hopefully, we are going to be able to get everyone together Saturday night to remove the hex."

"Do you need me?" Chris inquired.

"No," Kyra replied. "Just sit tight and I'll let you know how it goes."

...

December 21st: Kyra could not mask the look of concern on her face as she worked on her makeup in front of the mirror. "Who am I kidding?" she groaned.

Linda looked up from her laptop. "What's the problem, babe?"

Kyra sighed and turned away from the mirror. "Let's face it. This guy is used to Hollywood beauties, not a plain Jane like me."

"Plain Jane? You have to be kidding me," Linda laughed. "Look," she continued, "Beauty is always in the eye of the beholder, but for you it's been true of everyone you meet." Linda nodded. "Remember, it's easier for me to notice people looking at you than it is for you."

"Why is that?" Kyra asked.

"Because I'm insanely jealous," Linda grinned.

"Really?"

"Of course," Linda replied. "Strangers gaze at you when they think you're unaware. You have a kind of understated beauty, perhaps it is because you are so disarmingly unaware of your prettiness." Linda slipped behind Kyra and placed her hands on her shoulders. "Why do you waste your time with that makeup? Your skin is flawless. You are all about simplicity, making things easy, helping those around you to relax and be happy with what they have." Linda slowly turned Kyra around to face her. "Perhaps that is why your skin glows – it's your inner beauty that lights your eyes and softens your features. When you smile and laugh I can't help but smile along too, even if it is just on the inside." Linda's lips began moving forward. "To be in your company is to feel that I am somebody."

Linda initiated a long, soulful kiss. When her head retreated, she smiled. "Don't worry, babe. You will have no problem with this actor. Do you know why?"

"Why?"

Linda smiled. "Because you DO get better looking every day."

•••

Kyra had never been claustrophobic before, but in the almighty swell of humanity she felt the panic rise in her chest. When they moved she had to also and if her feet failed to keep up she risked being trampled underfoot.

Kyra took in the throng around her as best she could. It seemed that TVcon was much more than a few actors from canceled shows signing autographs. Besides TV characters, there were people dressed as comic book characters, movie heroes, and creatures that were totally unknown to her. The people flowed like rivers, never stopping for obstacles but swirling around them. On a day like this, crammed in with more bodies than she could count, Kyra tilted her head to the sky. The empty blue gave her the strength just to walk at the pace of the crowd and bottle her claustrophobia inside her chest.

Kyra always believed that the media conditioned humans to crave the spotlight, but by the look and feel of this mass of joyous humanity, the argument could be made that people were actually happiest when part of a crowd. She dismissed her claustrophobia for a moment and considered how this may be a great topic for Linda to publish – how people love to work together, achieve a common goal and cheer each other on. She took a deep breath and shook her head. Crowd behavior was a topic for a different day and a different paper. Right now, she had to focus on getting inside and getting to Michael Carlino.

This was uncharted territory for Kyra. Thousands of fans—donning everything from Game of Thrones armor to X-Men uniforms descended on the Javitz Center. Kyra enjoyed television, but these folks jamming around her were fans, with a capital F, of a wide swath of pop culture[1] ranging from TV shows to superheroes to exclusive collectible merchandise. They showed up for autographs, celebrity sightings, and panels that offered them a way to get that much

1.   https://www.cnet.com/topics/culture/

closer to the things they loved. Some people dressed as Klingons and others just loved the craziness, the spectacle and the energy of so many people in one place having the time of their lives.

Kyra was finally able to gain a little elbow room when she reached the Madison Pavilion on the upper level. Her destination was autograph hall A - the place to go for a special memento from a variety of artists, authors, and actors from every area of popular culture. Kyra searched the wall map looking for a specific name. When she located her target in the huge hall, she breathed a sigh of relief that she had joined a line of only eight people- the shortest in the hall.

The celebrity she had come to see sat behind the table in all his splendor, complete with a red and white Burger Bomb shirt, the same uniform he wore behind the counter in the Extra Cheese sitcom.

Kyra scanned the fans in front of her and felt a burst of optimism – all males.

Michael Carlino smiled and bantered amiably with a middle-aged man and his ten-year old son after signing two photos.

It was Kyra's turn and at the moment of truth she began to panic. She had completely forgotten it was an autograph show. She had no photo to be signed – not even a scrap of paper. All Kyra had was an introduction. "Hi, Mr. Carlino. I'm a really big fan of yours."

Kyra took the twinkle in Carlino's eyes as a positive sign. He stood and extended his hand. "What's your name, beautiful?"

Score Kyra thought. "My name is Kyra, Mr. Carlino."

"Nice to meet you, Kyra." When he completed scanning Kyra's body he performed a second scan and scratched his head. "What do you want me to sign?"

Kyra covered her mouth with her hand. "I'm so embarrassed. I was so excited about meeting you I forgot to bring anything to be autographed."

Carlino laughed. "That's okay sweetie, I love to get women excited." He pointed to the end of the long table. "Come around to this side and pull up a chair next to me. We'll talk while I'm signing and we'll figure out what I can sign for you."

Kyra got situated in the folding chair while Michael signed more autographs. Watching him engage the fans gave her an opportunity to assess her prey. He actually seemed to be very personable. He appeared to enjoy bantering with the people and he gave no one a brush off. He answered questions for as long as a person kept asking. Kyra also had a chance to assess his appearance. This was an easy analysis. Sitting next to her was a man in his fifties making a failing attempt to appear in his thirties, complete with the bad toupee and spray on tan.

Carlino handed a signed photo to another satisfied customer. He turned to Kyra and shook his head. "I'm never gonna get any time for you here. Why don't we get together later?"

That was easy, she thought. "Sure," Kyra gushed. She immediately regretted showing so much emotion as she realized Carlino would interpret the elation as being related to the opportunity to be with him.

"I have to be here until 6pm. I hope you can hold out until then." Carlino chuckled.

Kyra bit her lip. "It will be tough, but I'll try."

"I'm staying at the Remington Hotel on 59th Street. Why don't you come up to my room and we'll order room service?"

Kyra tried to keep him firmly on the hook while formulating a plan. "That sounds great. But it's going to be a mild night. Why don't we take a walk in the park first to work up an appetite?"

Carlino leaned over and rubbed Kyra's knee. "I can think of a fantastic way to work up an appetite and we don't even have to leave my room."

"We can save that for dessert," Kyra laughed.

"Okay, okay. We'll start with a walk in the park. What time?"

"How about 9:30 pm?"

"Great!" Carlino's hand was back on Kyra's knee. "Come up to room 615 and then we'll go to the park."

Kyra gently guided his hand off her knee. "How about we meet on the corner of 59th and 5th."

Carlino shrugged. "Suit yourself. I'll see you at 9:30."

Kyra smiled as she stood. "Until tonight then."

Kyra had almost reached the door when her exit was halted by Carlino's shout. "Hey Kyra. Don't bring anything to be signed. I know the perfect place on you to sign my name."

"I can't wait," she yelled back. When she pushed through the door into the hallway she gasped as if trying to catch her breath. "My God. What have I gotten myself into?"

Kyra was so intent on making her exit she didn't notice him standing next to the men's room door. At first glance it was easy to see why she would pay him no mind. His appearance was so pedestrian as to not be worth the trouble of a second look. He was clean shaven, average height, average build, with smart casual J-Crew clothing - the kind of guy that would melt into a line-up or a crowd like he was an extra, not really part of life at all. But a closer inspection told a different story. He was as pale as the full moon with wide, black sunken eyes staring like a cobra seeking it's prey. When Kyra was on the down escalator he moved for the first time when he raised his phone to his ear.

···

Linda adjusted the pillow on the sofa as she watched TV – but she wasn't really watching. She was too anxious regarding Kyra's adventure in Manhattan to concentrate on anything as mundane as a television show.

At the sound of the key, Linda's head snapped towards the door. "How did it go," she bubbled. "Tell me all about it."

Kyra turned left and walked directly down the hall toward the bathroom.

"Hey, where are you going?"

Kyra stuck her head out from the hallway. "Sorry, babe, but I have to jump into the shower immediately."

"Sounds like it really went well," Linda snickered.

Kyra entered the bathroom and raised her voice so Linda could hear. "That guy was the worst type of whorehound. As a matter of fact, he gives whorehounds a bad name."

"I see it went really well," Linda groaned.

"Just give me five minutes and I'll tell you the whole story," Kyra explained as she turned on the water.

Ten minutes later Kyra appeared from the hallway with a towel wrapped around her body, brushing out her wet hair. "As bad as it was being with that guy, things actually went incredibly well."

Linda perked up on the sofa. "Don't tell me you actually pulled it off."

Kyra smiled. "I did."

"You're incredible," Linda gushed. "How did you get him to agree to be part of the hex removal ceremony?"

"Well," Kyra bit her lip. "I didn't exactly tell him about that."

"What?"

"Look," Kyra explained. "I was lucky enough to meet him, get him interested in me and have him agree to meet me tonight. I didn't want to press my luck."

"So, what does he think he's doing tonight?" Linda asked.

"This letch just thinks he's going to score with me. He wanted to meet in his hotel room, but I said I wanted to take a walk in the park first before going to his room."

"So, you're just going to walk him into the middle of Serena Duval and the coven and spring this on him."

"Do you have any better ideas?"

Linda shook her head. "No babe, I don't – and you really did good. If you just think back to a couple of days ago when Mike told us about this Carlino guy, it's amazing that we are going to have him in the same place as Serena tonight."

"And there's no way I'm going to let him off the hook tonight," Kyra vowed. "Even if I have to promise him the ride of his life back in his hotel room."

"That's my girl," Linda smiled. "Always thinking of the team before herself." Linda rose from the sofa and gently pulled on the towel wrapped around Kyra, allowing it to drop to the floor. "How about coming to my room now," she whispered, "and giving me the ride of my life."

Kyra took Linda's hand and headed to the bedroom. "You're such a whorehound," she purred.

•••

Linda checked to make sure her feet were behind the yellow tactile strip at the edge of the platform before she leaned over and peered into the dark tunnel. It was only a five to ten-minute ride from the Vernon-Jackson subway station into Midtown Manhattan, but first a train had to appear.

Linda returned to the bench and paced in front of Kyra. "Okay, let's go over this one more time."

"Come on, we've been over the plan ten times," Kyra grumbled.

"One more time," Linda pled. "Just humor me."

"Ok," Kyra sighed. "You go to the park and meet with Serena and her witches at 9pm. I meet Mr. Wonderful at 9:30pm and we walk to the park to rendezvous with you and Serena."

"Correct," Linda nodded. "Then we drop the bombshell on Carlino and get the curse removed."

"Hex," Kyra corrected.

"Don't you start that now," Linda warned.

"Anyway," Kyra continued. "Don't forget to text me when it is okay for my date and me to enter the park. I don't want to spend any more time alone with this guy than I absolutely have to."

"Don't worry, babe, I'll send the text."

The progressively loud rumbling and light from the tunnel announced the arrival of the train. Ten minutes later Kyra and Linda stood on the southwest corner of 59th Street and 5th Avenue.

"Wow!" Kyra exclaimed. "What a mild night for late December."

"Yeah," Linda agreed. "I just hope it doesn't rain."

"Don't jinx us – or should I say hex us," Kyra snickered.

"Very funny," Linda moaned.

Linda leaned in and planted a quick peck on Kyra's lips. "See you later, babe. Watch for my text."

"Good luck," Kyra grinned. "See you later."

Kyra watched Linda disappear into the throng on Fifth Avenue. Suddenly, panic set in as she hustled into a coffee shop. There was still almost an hour before her scheduled street corner meeting with Carlino, but she didn't want to take any chances. Just in case he appeared on the street very early she did not want to be in his crosshairs."

The foot traffic on Fifth Avenue began to thin as Linda moved north. There were still plenty of people on the sidewalk, however, when she crossed 65th Street. When she turned into the park on the foot path between 65th and 66th Streets, the setting changed to one of a dimly lit path and no other people.

The environment was creepy to say the least and Linda's anxiety grew as she moved deeper into the park. Her anxiety transitioned to fear when the figure of a large, dangerous-looking man appeared in the dim light on the path walking towards her. She considered turning and running away but before she took flight she noticed the man was walking a very small dog. Her fears were instantly allayed with the thought that she never heard of any muggers who conducted their business while walking a tiny Maltese.

When Linda crossed paths with the man it turned out the only danger came from the tiny pooch, who growled menacingly and snapped in the direction of Linda's leg.

"Be nice, Cuddles," the huge man admonished his pet in a very high effeminate voice.

Linda shook her head and kept advancing into the park. She came to a fork in the path, and as per Serena's directions she stayed on the left side of the path. She continued for about a hundred yards until she noticed the terrain rise steeply to her right. At the top of this rise was a thick cluster of trees. The trees were so dense that even in December it was difficult to see beyond them.

Even with her athletic build, Linda was breathing heavily when she reached the top of the rise. She peered through the branches and could see activity in the clearing. There appeared to be no alternative, so she pushed forwards through the layers of branches, sustaining scratches on her hands and right cheek, and a small tear on the right side of her jacket. When she pushed through to the clearing she was greeted by a familiar voice.

"You're right on time," Serena Duval observed. "I appreciate punctuality."

Linda assessed her damage as she returned the greeting. "Hello, Serena. I wish you would have told me how difficult it was to get in here."

Serena howled with delight.

"What's so funny?" Linda fumed. "I'm all scratched up."

"If you had followed my directions," Serena chuckled and pointed to her right. "You would have seen that there was an entrance into this clearing about fifty yards further down the path."

"Oh well," Linda sighed. "There's no use crying over some scratches."

"So, I assume you're not alone," Serena remarked.

"Don't worry," Linda assured. "Kyra and the direct descendant will be along at 10pm."

"Good," Serena nodded. "And the young man affected by the hex?"

"What about him?"

"When will he arrive?"

"What?" Linda wailed. "You never said anything about Chris having to be here."

"Well, of course he has to be here," Serena snapped. "How can a hex be removed without the affected person being present."

"Well, excuse me," Linda barked. "How would I know that. I'm not the witch – you are!"

"Well honey," Serena replied. "You can be angry at me if you want but that doesn't change the situation. If that young man isn't present this is all a big waste of time – and I'm not refunding any of my fee."

Linda turned her back on Serena and grabbed her phone. "Hey, where are you right now?"

"I'm still at the coffee shop," Kyra replied. "What's wrong?"

"Plenty! Witch Hazel just dropped the bomb on me that Chris has to be here or the curse can't be broken."

"I'll call him," Kyra volunteered. "He knows me better. He lives in Queens so maybe our luck will hold out and he'll be able to make it to the park fast." Kyra did not wait for Linda's response. "See you soon, babe."

Kyra ran through her contacts until she reached Chris's name. "Hey Chris, it's Kyra Thomas."

"Dr. Thomas," Chris gushed. "Is it over? Did everything go well?"

"We're just having a little technical difficulty."

"What's that mean?" Chris groaned.

"It means that you have to be at the hex removal ceremony."

"What?" Chris bellowed. "No one told me..."

Kyra cut him off. "What's done is done and that's not important anymore. What is important is for you to get to Central Park as quickly as possible."

"It's gonna take me a couple of hours at least," Chris lamented. "By the time I get the bus to the train station..."

Kyra cut him off again. "Chris, we can't fool around. Call a God damn Uber – I'll pay for it."

"Where specifically am I going?"

"5th Avenue between 65th and 66th Streets. There's a footpath there to enter the park. Once you get there call me and I will guide you the rest of the way."

"Okay, Dr. Thomas, I'll see you as soon as possible."

Back in the park, Linda grabbed her phone and read the text –
CHRIS IS ON HIS WAY!

Serena was mingling with some of the coven while waiting for the
rest of the Manhattan witches to arrive. Linda approached with the
good news. "Chris will be here," she assured.

"Wonderful!" Serena beamed. "I'm still waiting for a couple of
people before we start."

Linda looked around at the ten women assembled in the clearing.
They looked like costume store witches complete with long black robes
adorned with stars and half-moons. Most of them carried wands that
had a plastic star attached to the tip. The only touch missing was the
pointy witch hat.

Linda turned to Serena. "Aside from removing the curse..."

"Hex," Serena cut in.

"I know – hex," Linda snarled. "Besides removing the hex, what else
are you doing tonight?"

"Our ceremony celebrates the Winter Solstice," Serena began.
"December 21st is significant because witches following the wheel of
the year start their midwinter celebrations on this date."

"What's the wheel of the year?" Linda asked.

"The wheel of the year is the cyclical calendar of festivals that
modern pagans celebrate. The wheel symbolizes the continuous
turning of time and mirrors nature's cycles of death and rebirth.
Traditionally, the festivities began on the longest night of the year and
celebrated the lengthening days and return of light. The yule festivities
stretched 12 days while its celebrants feasted and burned yule logs. This
coven, like most modern witches, don't have the time to celebrate for
twelve days – they limit their celebrations to December 21st."

A voice from behind ended Serena's description. "Hi Serena, good
to see you again."

Serena spun around. "Oh, hi Elena, good to see you." Serena placed her hand on Linda's shoulder. "This is my friend Linda – she will be joining us tonight."

"That's great," Elena smiled. "Nice to meet you."

"Same here," Linda replied.

"I have to start making preparations," Serena said. "Perhaps you have some questions for Elena," Serena suggested.

Linda shrugged. "What do you get out of this tonight, Elena?"

"The Solstice connects me with my ancestry. It is important to me to acknowledge the season change. Like nature, there are similar shifts and rebirths that occur inside me. Growing up I shared these rituals with my grandmother. I identify as a witch and I learned it all from my grandmother. I just recently found out that my great, great grandmother was a healer."

Linda stared at this woman spewing these profound magical words. She looked like any one of a million other forty-something suburban housewives."

"I see we have a newbie here tonight."

"This is Linda," Elena said as she continued the introduction. "And this is Marissa."

Linda was momentarily stunned. The woman walking over could have graced any billboard or magazine cover, but she was better than those two dimensional photoshopped models. She glided over with the slight breeze billowing her robe. Linda immediately realized that much of her beauty lay in her color. Burnt Sienna never looked so beautiful on a woman. With black hair of wool and her head held high, she waltzed over with an effortless saunter and extended her hand. When her eyes met Linda's she smiled. So beautiful it was like the stars themselves, decided to rest behind the soft cushion of her lips.

"Hi, I'm Marissa, very nice to meet you."

"Same here," Linda stammered, still smitten by the beauty before her.

Elena broke the ice. "Linda was just asking me what I get out of this ceremony."

"That's an easy one," Marissa remarked. "I observe the Solstice to honor rebirth, to observe stillness between the end of one cycle and the beginning of a new cycle. This ceremony also allows me to celebrate my being in a world that is trying to deny and erase the existence of trans and gender nonconforming folk. The ceremony brings power to the present moment, it's how we celebrate being alive and initiate change.

"I'm sorry," Linda gulped. "You're transgender?"

"yes, I am," Marissa crowed.

"You're so beautiful. Have you had the surgery?"

"No, and I have no intention of having the surgery. I am completely secure in who I am – a beautiful woman who happens to have a big dick." Marissa threw her head back and roared at her remark. Linda didn't really know what to say.

Serena supplied relief to the uncomfortable moment. "I'm going to get started with the ceremony. When we're done, hopefully your friends will be here and we will move on with the agenda."

"Sounds good to me," Linda nodded.

Linda stood off to the side while Serena walked into the middle of a circle of twelve robed women. "Remember, sisters," she began. "Solstice celebrations needn't be overly complicated, and you don't have to spend a lot of money to observe Solstice. If you can't make it to the ceremony remember to go to my website where you can find a very reasonably priced online ceremony."

Linda smiled. There was always time for a commercial.

"If this is your first time celebrating Solstice," Serena continued, "know that your first time is your rebirth. You are stepping onto the wheel, and you are stepping into that liminal space between time, between worlds. Let this be the beginning of your rebirth and let it be meaningful."

The circle of witches began moving counterclockwise around Serena, who provided commentary to the dance. "We pay tribute to nature and all of its wondrous mysteries."

The dance was now joined by a song:

Earth my body, water my blood, air my breast and fire my spirit.

The dancing and chanting went on and on. Every now and then Serena would break in with some special words. "In honor of our lady of the moon on this night when the full moon rides high in the sky as a symbol of our love and respect for the goddess we meet below the full moon to share our joy of life and to thank our lord and lady for all she has given us and for all that we have."

Serena waved her wand over her head. "Now begins our magical rite."

Linda watched the festivities and didn't really know what to think. The ceremony was supposed to be so solemn and rustic in their attempt to become one with nature, yet they were all standing in the middle of Midtown Manhattan. While all the chants and dances in honor of nature and the moon were taking place the sounds of the city were audible all around them. Horns honked and sirens blared throughout the commutation with nature. Even a jazz band began playing somewhere in the park nearby. Linda found it all ridiculous, but the distractions did not deter Serena and the coven. Linda found it especially ironic when the loudest sirens sounded just as Serena began leading the group in the serenity chant.

Back on 59th Street Kyra saw him through the throng of New Yorkers and tourists enjoying the sights and sounds of the holidays in the City. She curled her lip as she watched his approach. He wasn't a bad looking man, despite that beaky nose. He was beautifully shaven, something Kyra noticed about men, and his olive skin looked like felt. He dressed expensively, or at least attempted to look that way, with a lot of gold glitter. Kyra sighed. He would actually be a reasonably attractive package if he didn't come across like the worst type of lounge lizard, and if he could only keep his big fat mouth shut, a big fat mouth that was making itself known.

"Hey, hey," he said with a lip-smacking grin. "You look ravishing – and if there weren't all these people around I would ravage you."

Carlino leaned in for a kiss, but Kyra quickly turned her head changing the target from her lips to her cheek.

It didn't take Kyra long to realize that Carlino had spent some time in the hotel bar before coming to meet her. His eyes were slightly out of focus, his speech a bit slurred.

"Whew!" he gasped. "That was quite a walk. Why don't we go back to my room now?"

"Please, Mr. Carlino, I really want to walk through the park first."

"Okay, okay," he replied. "We'll go for a walk, and then it will be back to my room for some rest."

Kyra stepped into the crosswalk when the light turned green. Carlino put his arm around Kyra and pulled her close to him.

"Easy, Hercules," Kyra protested. "How about letting me breathe a little."

"Sorry," he laughed. "But you're so cute. I just want to eat you up."

"Let's just wait until we're alone," Kyra declared. "I'm shy about these public displays of affection."

"Whatever you say, honey," Carlino said as he planted another kiss on Kyra's cheek.

Kyra couldn't get to 65th Street quick enough. She saw the entrance to the foot path and guided Carlino into the park. Immediately, Kyra realized she was in trouble. The dimly lit desolate walkway was the perfect environment for a Romeo like Carlino. Slowly his arm slid off her shoulder and down her arm. He quickly transitioned to resting his hand on the side of her waist but an instant later that same hand was getting a workout squeezing her breast.

"You like that, don't you baby," Carlino drooled.

Kyra had come too far to blow the whole operation now, so a creep's hand on her breast wasn't going to get a big reaction – she just took a deep breath and dealt with it, but she also was not going to wait a second longer for Linda's text.

"Just a minute, I have to check this text," Kyra lied. She quickly texted Linda: *We're here – Where are you? – Help!*

The reply text was quick. *Bear left at the fork in the path. Keep going for a few hundred feet. I'll meet you."*

Carlino's hand found its way right back to Kyra's breast as she guided him to the left at the fork.

"How much more do you want to walk?" he asked. "I can tell you're getting excited."

Kyra fought the urge to vomit. "I love the park, don't you? Just a little further and we'll head back."

"I'm ready when you are, baby – for anything!"

Again, the urge to puke began to dominate. Before Kyra barfed a figure on the road ahead settled her stomach.

"Kyra, is that you?"

Kyra played along with Linda's charade. "Linda," she sang. "What are you doing here?"

"I was just attending a meeting with some friends. Come check it out."

Kyra looked at Carlino. "It will just take a minute. Let's go with Linda."

"Who's your friend?" Linda asked.

"Forgive me for being rude. This is Michael."

"Hi Michael. I'm Linda."

Carlino took Linda's hand. "And you're one hot dish too."

"Come on," Linda directed. "Everyone is in the clearing beyond the trees."

"More hotties?" Carlino slurred. "I hope they are as hot as you two."

Linda glanced at Kyra and rolled her eyes. "Hotter, Michael. We are the ugly ducklings."

"Let's go ladies."

When the trio entered the clearing, the circle was still dancing and chanting while Serena waved her wand in the middle.

"I could do without the old bat in the middle," Carlino yammered, "but some of the dancers are okay. Let's see who wants to join us back in my room."

Kyra grabbed Carlino's hand. "Michael, come with me over to those trees. I have something very important I need to tell you in private."

"Whatever you say, beautiful. I'll go anywhere with you in private."

"I'll keep my eye on you," Linda whispered before Kyra disappeared with Carlino behind a large tree.

Ten minutes and one incredible story later, Michael Carlino sat on a large rock and scratched his head. "I get it. This is one of those hidden camera shows, right?"

"Like I told you, Michael, this is probably nothing, but it doesn't hurt anyone to go through with this hex removal ceremony."

Carlino laughed heartily. "And my great great great great great great grandmother was some demented witch who cursed a cop in 1692, and this curse has been killing cops ever since then. That's what you expect me to believe."

"Something like that," Kyra nodded.

"What the hell," Carlino sighed. "I'll bite – let's go remove a curse." Carlino put his arm around Kyra and pulled her close to him. "But then it's back to my room."

"Sure, of course," she gasped. "Let's get back there and get this going."

When Kyra returned to the clearing the circle was taking a break from dancing. Kyra took the opportunity to make an announcement.

"Serena, this is Michael Carlino. He's a direct descendant of the witch who hexed Chris."

"Where is the young man?" Serena asked.

"He just texted me," Kyra replied. "He's five minutes away."

The voice from the far side of the clearing was oozing with excitement. "Michael Carlino – I don't believe it, it's Michael Carlino."

Carlino took one look at the statuesque beauty headed his way and Kyra was instantly dumped into second place in the Michael Carlino sweepstakes.

"Oh my God," Marissa fawned. "I can't believe this. I love you."

"Well, I do seem to have that effect on women," Carlino boasted.

"Extra Cheese is my favorite show of all time, and believe me, you do get better looking every day."

Kyra squinted slightly. "Weren't you a bit young when that show was on?"

"I bought every season on Amazon Prime." Marissa clarified. "And Michael was my favorite character." Marissa looked at Kyra. "He is just so sexy!"

"He's the sexiest," Kyra deadpanned.

Carlino raised his hands. "Steady ladies, there's enough of me to go around." He winked at Marissa. "And you, my gorgeous darling, are cordially invited back to my room when I finish removing this curse."

"I'd love to, Michael," Marissa sang.

Kyra looked at Linda. "Wow, that was a quick brush off."

"No, no," Carlino interjected. "The more the merrier."

"Wonderful," Kyra groaned.

"Hey, look who's here," Linda exclaimed.

Chris Bennington trotted into the clearing breathing heavily. "Did I make it in time, Dr. Thomas?"

"Perfect timing, Chris, we're just about to get started."

"Dr. Thomas?" Carlino blurted. "You're a doctor?"

"Yeah," Kyra shot back. "I'm a doctor. Is there a problem with that?"

Carlino shook his head. "No problem. It's kind of kinky actually."

Kyra bit her lip. "Can we get on with this please."

"The circle has to perform one more song to the moon and the we will be done," Serena stated.

Carlino glanced up to the sky. "Moon – what moon?"

The reason for the moon's sudden disappearance became obvious with the clap of thunder followed by the downpour. Umbrellas began popping up all around the circle. Serena actually brought a spare umbrella that she tossed to Linda. "That's the amazing thing about New York City," Linda declared.

"What's amazing?" Kyra asked as she squeezed under the umbrella.

"As soon as it begins raining in the city everyone seems to have an umbrella. They just seem to appear out of nowhere." She nodded toward the coven. "Even the circle of witches had umbrellas and the head witch even brought a spare."

"Room for one more, ladies," Carlino inquired as he thrust his pelvis into Linda's butt.

"Hey!" Linda shouted.

"Sorry, but I had to get out of that rain."

Elena called out to Serena. "This isn't going to stop soon. The rest of the girls and I are going to call it a night. Thanks for everything, Serena."

"Good night, girls," Serena sang.

Carlino called out to Marissa. "Hey beautiful. I hope you're not abandoning me."

Marissa smiled. "I wouldn't think of it."

"Hey everyone," Carlino announced. "Why don't we all retreat to my hotel room where you can do that voo doo that you do do and remove this hex. Then I can work my magic with the ladies."

"What magic are you referring to," Serena asked.

Carlino waved his hand dismissively. "Don't worry about it. It doesn't concern you."

Fifteen minutes later Michael Carlino led the parade into room 615.

"Everyone settle down please," Serena growled. "I can't stay here all night." She waited a moment until there was complete quiet inside the room. "This spell I am about to perform is performed to remove any curse."

"I think you mean hex," Linda remarked.

Kyra punched Linda's arm. "Stop!"

"Sorry," Linda shrugged. "I couldn't resist."

"If there are no further interruptions," Serena grumbled. "I will continue. The only difference is with a lineage hex a direct descendant of the witch who placed the original hex must be present. In this case, I thank Mr. Carlino for his participation."

"It's my pleasure," Michael mocked. "I couldn't think of anything better to do on a Saturday night in New York City than remove a hex."

"I can think of something better to do," Marissa purred.

"Later sweetie," Michael replied. "Let the wicked witch of the west do her stuff and then I'll show you my magic wand later."

"I can't wait," Marissa grinned.

"Can we have quiet – now!" Serena scolded. "To start with, this spell may be worked at any time. You don't have to wait for a particular phase of the Moon. You don't have to wait for a specific day of the week. And you certainly don't have to bother with those annoying ceremonial calculations that involve figuring the proper hour, minute, and second. This spell works well no matter when it's performed. And since you're more than likely using it to remove some nasty crap from someone's life, waiting around for the planets to cooperate simply isn't an option. That's good news. Another thing is that this spell is absolutely foolproof. There's no way you can screw it up, and you don't have to be a magical genius to get results. All you have to do is have the descendant present, follow the directions, know that you're going to get exactly what you asked for, and relax. That's good news too." Serena cleared her throat. "Now then, while size usually doesn't matter, it actually does here."

Michael leaned in close to Marissa. "That's not true," he whispered. "Size does matter."

Serena glared at Michael. "Size matters as far as the candles go. Because they must burn until they extinguish themselves, it's in your best interest to avoid using votive candles. We will use small tapers instead." Serena again fixed her gaze on Michael. "I will assist the direct descendant to perform this spell. There's good reason for this. No matter how intimately you're connected to the person you have in mind, there's no way you can truly feel their angst and fury or the full impact of those emotions on their life. And since the power of the spell feeds upon those emotions and the specific way that they affect the person in question, the effects of the spell simply aren't as strong when performed by anyone but a direct descendant." Serena scanned the audience in the room. "With all of this out of the way, let's get started." She looked toward Chris. "You'll be amazed at how easy it is, how well it works, and how quickly your life returns to normal!"

Knock – Knock

"Damn it!" Kyra mumbled. "What now?" Frustration was setting in. They had somehow gotten this plan to work to the point where they were in a room with a direct descendant of Katherine Harris and were about to go through the ceremony to remove the hex, whether it was real or not. She didn't want anything to stop the progress. "Keep going," she urged. "I'll see who it is."

The first thing Kyra noticed was the pale complexion around the black sunken eyes. A much greater impression, however, was made by the barrel of the 9mm semi-auto pistol pointed at her face. The sinister figure with the gun remained silent. Verbal direction was supplied by a voice behind him. "Please move into the room young lady."

Kyra backed slowly into the room. Linda was the first to notice the new visitors. "Oh my God! What the hell is going on? Why are you here, Goff?"

George Goff emerged from behind the gunman taking measured steps with the assistance of his cane. He smiled and politely bowed his head. "I'm flattered that you remember me, Miss. Now, would everyone please move to the corner of the room and place your hands above your heads."

Kyra joined the group assembled in the corner and raised her hands high in the air. "What are you here for, Goff?"

"I'm here to preserve my heritage," Goff replied. "To make sure the right thing is done."

"What the hell are you talking about?" Linda blurted.

George Goff leaned heavily on his cane. "I'm sorry, but I can't recall your name, Miss."

"Linda."

"What religion are you, Linda?"

"Catholic."

"Well," Goff began. "in that case, I'm sure you can understand the concept of a messiah."

Linda squinted and shook her head. "What on earth are you talking about?"

"Jesus Christ is your Messiah – your savior."

"What's your point?" Linda growled.

"For the Sons of Massapequa," Goff said. "You might say that Tackapausha, the Massapequa chief is our Messiah."

Linda still did not understand. "So?"

"Just as you have the crucifixion of Christ as the focal point of your religion, we have the execution of Katherine Harris as ours."

Kyra took her eyes off the gun to join the questioning. "But you just said the Massapequa chief was your messiah, not Katherine Harris."

"That's correct, young lady," Goff replied. "But what happened at that execution is the centerpiece of our faith. Tackapausha and some of the Dutch coven were at the execution and what he said are our holiest words."

Linda stared at Chris. "I don't get it. You had all these specific memories. Why didn't you tell us about the Native American Chief being at the execution?"

"Don't be angry with the young man," Goff chimed in. "He wouldn't have any memory because Baltis Van Steyer wasn't there."

"What do you mean he wasn't there?" Linda scoffed. "Chris said Baltis Van Steyer brought Katherine Harris to the gallows."

"He did," Goff agreed. "But Van Steyer was so sickened by an innocent woman being put to death that he left the scene before the execution and before Tackapausha revealed himself."

"So, what profound words did your messiah utter?" Linda asked.

"As the rope was being placed around Katherine's neck, she again screamed out the content of the hex. Tackapausha then shouted to the assembled crowd that this unjust execution would be avenged through all time by the descendants of Katherine Harris, and should a descendant exercise the bad judgement to remove the hex, that descendant would face dire consequences and another descendant would have the power to renew the hex. The chief then said that he sealed his words with his own blood."

Goff took a deep breath. "Tackapausha took a knife and thrust it into his own heart."

"This is the 21st century, Goff." Linda remarked. "Why is it so damn important to you to keep this curse going?"

"Hex, not curse," Serena corrected.

"Why don't you shut up," Linda growled.

"She's right," Goff remarked. "The correct terminology is hex, but that's not important. You have to understand that to the Sons of Massapequa, the words of Tackapausha and the Katherine Harris hex are like the pilot light of our spirituality. If that pilot light is extinguished, so are we." Goff's voice took on a somber tone. "And I will not allow that to happen."

Linda again directed her wrath toward Serena. "You really set us up good, didn't you – you bitch!"

"What are you talking about?" Serena shot back.

"You took our money and tipped off these assholes."

"You're out of your mind," Serena gasped. "I've heard of the Sons of Massapequa, but I knew nothing about these men or their beliefs."

"So, what happens now?" Kyra asked. "What are you going to do to us?"

"Nothing," Goff shrugged. "I'm a civilized man. I just don't want any interference with the natural course of events. My colleague will tie you up and leave you here unharmed while we leave with Mr. Carlino."

"Wait a minute!" Carlino stammered. "This is enough craziness for one night. Check that – it's enough craziness for a lifetime. I'm not going anywhere with you and your goon!"

Goff sighed. "I do hope you will reconsider, Mr. Carlino. If you come with us you will be our guest until the natural conclusion, and then you will be free to go."

"What the hell is the natural conclusion?" Carlino blurted.

"He means when I get killed," Chris clarified.

Goff shook his head. "I'm very sorry, young man, but sometimes nature can be unkind to the innocent. Just ask Katherine Harris."

"Screw you and your nature," Carlino bellowed. "I aint going nowhere!"

Goff sighed again. "The alternative is for my associate to shoot you right now. The choice is yours."

Michael Carlino made many different sounds but no intelligible words came out of his mouth.

Goff addressed his gunman. "Give me the gun. Get the rope we left at the door and make our friends comfortable."

Goff kept the pistol trained on the group in the corner of the room while using the cane in his left hand to maintain his balance. Goff's silent assistant went to work and very efficiently tied the arms and legs of Kyra, Linda, Serena, and Marissa. With their intent to leave with Calino, the creepy henchman tied only his hands behind his back. Only Chris remained to finish the job. The dark sunken eyes focused on Chris and began moving towards him with rope in hand. As the man reached for Chris, he was startled by Chris's shout. "Screw this! Let's see nature do its job right now!"

Chris vaulted over the bed and sprinted toward Goff. Goff pulled desperately on the trigger but the pistol misfired, with the only sound emanating from the firearm being harmless clicking. Chris lowered his shoulder and threw a running block that would have made his high school football coach proud. Goff went flying backwards, his cane flew through the air to the left and the gun flew to the right and hit the door to the room. Chris scrambled to his feet and dove towards the gun. Goff's goon intercepted him before he could grab the firearm as they both rolled on the floor. Chris kicked the gun along the floor to the other side of the room. When the man made a move to retrieve the firearm, Chris bolted through the door and into the hallway.

"Help, we need help!" Chris's voice faded as he reached the end of the hall.

Goff had retrieved his cane and struggled to his feet. "Get the gun and let's go," he growled.

The henchman tucked the gun in his waistband before placing Goff's arm around his shoulder. At the doorway, Goff turned his head to the room. "This isn't over. There are other ways to prompt nature."

"What do we do now?" Carlino asked.

"I guess we wait for help," Linda replied. "At least you can still move around. Why don't you go to the door and look out for help."

Carlino shook his head. "No way! That goon with the gun may still be out there, and with my luck it won't misfire this time."

It seemed like an hour, but it was really only four minutes before Chris appeared at the door. "The police have been notified," he announced as he untied Carlino's hands. "Where are those guys?" he asked as he began untying Kyra.

"Who cares?" Linda blurted. "As long as they are gone."

The uniform cops with guns drawn came storming into the room first followed by the detectives who displayed much less drama in their entry. The questioning went on for over an hour as the investigators tried to make sense out of a psychiatrist, a college professor, a washed-up actor, a witch, a rookie NYPD rubber gun squad member and a trans gender male being victimized by a man from some secret society in the actor's hotel room. In the end, the lead detective said that Goff likely went home and that the Nassau County Police Department would have no problem picking him up. He then took one last look at the odd assemblage in the room, shook his head and mumbled, "Happy Holidays."

Michael Carlino collapsed on the bed and moaned. "I need a drink!" He stared up at the ceiling and articulated his desire. "What do you say, Kyra? Why don't we ask everyone else to leave us to cozy up to a drink and each other? How does that sound, sweetie?"

The lack of response made him lift his head to seek out Kyra. "What the fuck!" he bellowed.

The adrenaline of the incident had finally drained from Kyra as she collapsed into Linda's arms. Despite their progressive attitudes, Kyra and Linda shied away from public displays of affection, but being tied up with a gun pointed at them was a good formula for throwing caution to the wind. Very quickly their lips were locked in a long soulful kiss and Michael Carlino felt worse than when the gun had been pointed at him.

Carlino shot upright on the bed. "You mean you two are....."

Kyra and Linda were too involved with each other to respond to the inquiry, but Marissa climbed into the bed behind Carlino and placed a soothing hand on his back. "It's okay, Michael," Marissa reassured.

Carlino's mood immediately brightened. "At least there is one lovely lady here who shows an interest in me." He turned in the bed and stroked Marissa's cheek. "You and me, baby," he whispered, "We're gonna have a wild time."

"I can't wait," Marissa giggled.

Serena clapped her hands like an angry teacher in front of a rowdy classroom. "Can we please finish this," she urged.

Linda released Kyra to express surprise at Serena's direction. "Why do we have to finish this? We have our answer."

"What do you mean, babe?" Kyra asked.

Linda rolled her eyes. "Was I the only one in this room. Our boy Chris here took the heroic action of rushing Goff and the gun jammed."

Kyra tilted her head and squinted. "So?"

"So," Linda gushed. "The situation was set up perfectly for Chris to be killed in the line of duty before he separated from the department and it didn't happen. This curse is bogus after all."

"Hex." Serena corrected again.

"Please shut up, Serena," Linda huffed.

"Hey, she's right, Chris," Kyra added. "You were right in the line of fire but it didn't happen."

Chris scratched his head. "I guess you're right."

"We shouldn't take any chances," Serena jumped in. "We should finish this?"

"Why?" Kyra asked.

"First of all," Serena began. "You already paid me and I don't want you bothering me for a refund. Second, and most important. We don't know if what happened with the misfire was a coincidence and that Chris is still destined to die."

"I say let's finish," Chris exclaimed. "That's what we're here for, right?"

Kyra looked at Linda and nodded. "It's fine with us."

Michael rubbed his index finger slowly along Marissa's lips. "Let's get this over with. Marissa and I have a big night ahead of us."

"Okay, everyone stay on the side of the room near the bed," Serena directed. "I will use the top of the dresser as the altar."

"Will that work?" Chris asked.

"Of course," Serena replied. "An altar can be anything," she smiled. "Like I always say, It's not the wand that makes the magic, it's the witch waving it."

Carlino was comfortably stretched out on the bed with his back against the headboard. He pulled Marissa close to him and snickered. "That's funny because I say the same thing."

"What?" Marissa grinned.

"It's not the magic wand that's important, it's the magician using it." He suggestively pointed to his crotch.

"Oh, you're bad!" Marissa bubbled.

"Just wait and see how bad I can be sweetheart."

In the two chairs next to the bed Kyra and Linda looked at each other. "I hope we don't act this way with each other," Linda remarked.

"Please," Kyra shook her head. "If I thought for a minute we were like him it would be time to turn asexual."

"You don't know what you're gonna be missing, ladies," Carlino heckled.

"Please," Serena scolded. "I need your complete attention." She began removing items from her bag and placing them on the dresser while providing a narration. "First, we have a cookie sheet."

"I love cookies," Carlino cut in. "Whip up a batch of chocolate chip."

"You're a riot!" Marissa howled.

Kyra was not amused. She kicked the side of the bed. "Will you please shut up and let Serena do this."

"Okay, okay. Geez, no one has a sense of humor anymore."

Serena sneered in Carlino's direction before continuing her set up. "Now I will place on the cookie sheet one black candle, one brown candle, one white candle, and some table salt. The final ingredient is a large supply of negative energy."

"Where is that?" Linda asked.

Serena pointed to Chris. "This is why we are here. The young man is filled with many generations of negative energy." Serena began manipulating the candles. "I will begin at the center left-hand side of the cookie sheet and arrange the candles in a specific horizontal order – black, brown, then white." She grabbed the salt. "I shall sprinkle the salt to extend the line from the candles to a point about three-quarters of the way to the right edge of the pan." Serena leaned in closer for her next task. "I am now drawing an arrow tip with the salt at the end of the line and now I am using the salt to draw a circle around the arrow tip to encase it."

Serena pulled a notepad and pen out of her bag. She motioned with her index finger for Chris to approach the dresser. "Write your desire on the paper in large block letters." She turned to the audience by the bed. "In actuality, this desire can be anything – money, a new job, love, protection, good health – as long as it's something for which you have a need." Serena turned back to face Chris again. "But since we're breaking a hex here, simply write GOOD FORTUNE."

Serena folded the paper into thirds, then into thirds again. "I am now placing the paper inside the salt circle directly on top of the arrow tip."

Serena took a deep breath. "For the next part of the ceremony I must have the direct descendant."

Carlino leaned over and planted a kiss on Marissa's cheek. "It's showtime. Watch me do my stuff, baby." He bounced out of the bed and stood next to Serena like he had made an entrance on stage.

Serena handed Carlino a small cigarette lighter. Michael took the device and noted the printing on its side – *Have a Nice Day, Asshole.* "I like it," Carlino nodded.

"Your focus is important," Serena warned.

"Sorry."

"Okay," Serna continued. "Light the black candle and focus on all the nasty energy coming your way." Michael lit the candle as Serena's voice took on a more dramatic tone. "Focus on all the negative energy coming your way from your lineage. See all the harm it's done, the trouble it's caused, and feel your personal misery."

"Hey, I really didn't do anything to cause this," Carlino shrugged.

"Quiet!" Serena ordered. "Now, take a step further and feel your personal anger. Don't just become angry though. Let the fury consume you until you are absolutely and positively livid."

Carlino grit his teeth. "Oh man, I am really pissed," he hissed.

"Scream, stomp," Serena urged. "Whatever it takes to get you there."

Carlino stomped his feet on the carpet and screamed. "I'm mad as hell and I'm not gonna take it anymore!"

Kyra leaned into Linda and whispered. "Didn't I see that in a movie?"

"Ssshh," Linda admonished along with a quick poke in Kyra's side.

Serena nodded. "That was good, Mr. Carlino. Now, please repeat after me – *I name this black candle negativity.*"

"I name this black candle negativity," Michael repeated.

"Good," Serena pointed to the cookie tray. "Now light the brown candle." As Carlino moved forward with the lighter Serena continued with the instructions. "Take a deep breath and exhale slowly, releasing every particle of anger from your body."

Carlino overacted to the maximum. "I'm doing it – I'm doing it. I can feel it draining from me."

"When the detachment takes over," Serena continued, "feel the weight of your personal responsibility lighten."

Carlino broke from character. "Well, frankly, like I said, I don't feel responsible for this."

"Please, stay with the ceremony," Serena demanded. "Now, see the energy begin to transform into something neutral. Repeat after me again – *I name this candle transformation.*"

"I name this candle transformation."

Serena extended her hand toward the cookie tray. "Now light the white candle. See the energy transformation process as complete. There is nothing left but clear, bright, raw, pure energy. Energy that you can harness to remove this evil hex of your ancestors. Repeat after me – *I name this candle pure energy.*"

"I name this candle pure energy."

Serena pointed to the salt line in the tray. "With your eyes, follow the salt line from the candle to the circle and focus on Chris's desire to have this evil energy removed from him." Serena reached out and grabbed Carlino's forearm. "Visualization is very important here, for you not only need to vocalize your wishes, but you have to feel it happening."

Carlino closed his eyes. "I'm seeing it – halleluiah!"

Serena pushed forward. "As you can see, the candles are beginning to burn themselves out."

There was an uncomfortable silence in the room until the final white candle burned itself out. Once all the candles had extinguished themselves, Serena continued. "Mr. Carlino, please use the lighter on the folded paper and leave it in the circle until it burns to ash."

Linda felt she had to interrupt. "I hope we don't activate the sprinkler system."

"Good point," Serena nodded. "Chris, stand on a chair by that smoke detector on the wall and wave away any smoke coming that way. The paper is very small, so it should be quick, but it is imperative that the paper is completely reduced to ash."

"Okay," Serena noted. "The paper has reached the ash stage."

Everyone in the room breathed a collective sigh of relief at that fact that no alarm had been activated.

"Now, for the final stage of the ceremony," Serena declared. She handed Carlino a small plastic bag and a spoon. "Please collect the ash and salt and put those remnants into the bag. This is preparation for burial. Burying the items is the most important part of the hex removal because it grounds the dark magic. Once the burial is performed, things will begin the change immediately. There is no waiting period as is normal for other spells." Serena looked at Chris and smiled. "All that will be left is for you to live a long, happy life."

"Wait a minute," Carlino whined while holding his bag of ash and salt. "How the hell am I supposed to bury this on the 6th floor of a hotel?"

"The ability to improvise is crucial for casting an effective spell." Serena waved for everyone to follow her as she entered the bathroom. "Come on," she beckoned. Don't be shy. Everyone can fit."

Once everyone was inside the small bathroom Serena brought the ceremony to completion. "Repeat after me Mr. Carlino – *As I bury this ash and salt, so too is buried the evil magic brought forth by my ancestor.*"

"Whew, that's a long one." Carlino shook his head. "But I'll try." He cleared his throat. "I now bury this stuff and all the evil of my ancestor."

Serena rolled her eyes. "Close enough."

"Now what?" Carlino shrugged.

"What do you think?" Serena chastised. "You bury the items."

"Bury them how?"

Like I said, we have to improvise." Serena pointed to the toilet.

"You want me to flush it?" Carlino babbled.

"Trust me, it works," Serena assured.

"Oh well," Carlino shrugged. "You're the head witch." He sprinkled the contents of the bag into the water and pushed down the handle. The ash and salt began its slow spiral down until it disappeared into the bowels of the hotel's pipes.

Serena nodded. "It is done." She raised her eyebrows and extended her arm toward Carlino.

"What?" Carlino questioned.

"Say it!" Serena directed.

"Say what?"

"What I just said."

"What did you say?" Carlino mused. "I'm not a mind reader."

"Just say it is done, for God's sake," Linda growled.

"Sure beautiful," Carlino winked. "It is done."

Everyone moved back into the room and Carlino immediately assumed his previous position on the bed with his back up against the headboard. "So that's it, it's over?" he asked.

"Yes," Serena nodded. "The ceremony has concluded."

"And they paid you for this." Carlino shook his head. "What a scam. I guess I should have charged for being the ancestor to old evil grandma broom Hilda."

Only Marissa laughed at the comment. Carlino waved her over to him. "Come here, baby, and get comfortable with me on the bed." He glanced at Kyra and Linda. "You're still welcome to join us, but if not, I would ask you to join Kid Hex and Witch Hazel in making your exit." He stared into Marissa's eyes. "This gorgeous creature and I desire to be alone."

The foursome stopped on the corner of 59th Street and 5th Avenue. "Are you joining us on the train, Serena?" Linda asked.

"No, I have to get the PATH train to go back to Jersey. The rain has stopped and it's a beautiful night under a full moon, so I am just going to take a leisurely stroll down to Penn Station."

"Well, thanks very much for your help, and I apologize for thinking you set us up with those creeps," Linda smiled.

"That's okay," Serena smiled. "We had a happy ending."

Kyra and Chris echoed the sentiment "Yeah, thanks."

The trio reached the top of the 5th Avenue subway station stairs when Kyra abruptly stopped. "Wait a minute," she snarled. "Why were we thanking that witch. Maybe Carlino was right. We paid her a lot of money for her to light candles and spread salt around. How do we know this actually worked?"

"Oh, it worked," Chris said in a voice barely above a whisper.

"What?" Kyra bellowed.

Linda grabbed Chris's hand. "How do you know it worked, Chris?"

"They're gone," Chris shrugged.

"What's gone?" Linda questioned.

Chris smiled. "The memories."

"They're gone?" Kyra gasped.

"The moment that sleazy guy said it is done – they were gone."

"You don't remember anything?" Linda queried.

"Of course," he clarified, "I still remember the general stories I talked about since this happened, but the vivid detail in the actual memories has left me." Chris nodded. "I'm gonna be okay."

"That's fantastic," Kyra exclaimed. "I'm just sorry that creep Carlino is having his own happy ending with Marissa. I don't understand what she sees in that dope. I couldn't get his hands off me while we were walking to the park."

"Well," Linda laughed. "I don't think Mr. Carlino is having a happy ending."

"Why?" Kyra asked.

Linda pointed to the stairs. "Let's go down to the platform and I'll tell you all about it."

Back in Room 615 Michael Carlino was moving in for the kill. His tongue was exploring every inch of the inside of Marissa's mouth. Her witch's robe was long gone and Michael was slowly pushing her skirt aside as his hand methodically rose from Marissa's knee to the inner thigh to the precipice of paradise.

Suddenly, all the color drained from Michael Carlino's face. For the second time in the same evening a man burst out from Room 615 screaming for help.

EPILOGUE:

December 22nd: Kyra rejoiced as she stared at the headline in the New York Post – *ROOKIE COP FOILS HOTEL ROBBERY ATTEMPT IN ACTOR'S ROOM.*

The story was perfect in that it made Chris Bennington a hero without mentioning anything about witchcraft. Kyra looked through her phone contacts until she found the correct cell number. "Lieutenant Evans," she greeted. "I'm so sorry to bother you on a Sunday morning. But this is urgent."

"Who is this?" Mike Evans fumed.

"Dr. Thomas – the psychiatrist you met regarding the Chris Bennington case."

"I remember. What's up Dr. Thomas?"

"I just wanted to remind you that you will have my report on Chris tomorrow and that my report will find Chris Bennington perfectly fit for duty."

"Dr. Thomas," Evans sighed. "We've been through all this and you know the bottom line. Chris Bennington gets a medical disability tomorrow."

"Have you seen the New York Post today?" Kyra asked.

"No."

"Well, lieutenant, I strongly suggest you and your colleagues read today's paper before you make your final decision. That is, unless the NYPD is in the happy of terminating its heroes right after they save a life."

"What are you talking about?"

"Have a good day, Lieutenant," Kyra sang.

When she disconnected the call, Linda was waiting with a high five. "Way to go girl. That should do it."

Linda stroked her chin. "By the way, when you were telling me how that creepy Carlino had his hands all over you, what exactly did he do?"

Kyra smiled and grabbed Linda's hand. "Come with me and I'll show you every horrible thing he did to me."

"Was it really that bad?" Linda asked.

"Oh, it was horrible, you'll see," Kyra said as she closed the bedroom door.

•••

December 28th: "Hi Lieutenant Evans, It's Dr. Thomas. I just wanted to thank you for not terminating Chris Bennington. He's thrilled and I'm sure he's going to make a fine police officer."

"I hope you're right, Dr. Thomas. All we try to do is the right thing."

"I'm sure you do, Lieutenant, but I do have to say that it is a little surprising that the suspects from the other night were not captured. Chris told me that the detective who responded said that the Nassau County Police would pick them up easily when they went home."

"I checked with the detective, and obviously the perpetrators never went home. As a matter of fact," Evans continued, "their trail has momentarily gone cold."

"So, you have no idea where they are," Kyra snickered.

"Don't worry," Evans assured. "they'll turn up – they always do."

•••

The desk clerk smiled at the approaching guest. "May I help you sir?"

"Yes, I'm going to have to extend my stay a bit longer."

"How long?"

"At least a week."

"No problem, sir. I have you confirmed for the next week."

The guest began to depart, but stopped abruptly and turned back towards the clerk, balancing himself on his cane. "Is there a lot of snow this time of year in Iceland?"

About the Author

Robert L. Bryan is a law enforcement and security professional. He served twenty years with the New York City Transit Police and the New York City Police Department, retiring at the rank of Captain. Presently, Mr. Bryan is the Chief Security Officer for a New York State government agency. He has a B.S in criminal justice from St. John's University and an M.S. in security management from John Jay College of Criminal Justice. Additionally, Mr. Bryan is an Adjunct Professor in the Homeland Security Department and the Security Systems and Law Enforcement Technology Department for two New York Metropolitan area colleges. For more information about Mr. Bryan's other books, please visit his Amazon Author page: https://www.amazon.com/Robert-L.-Bryan/e/
B01LXUSALG?ref_=dbs_p_ebk_r00_abau_000000